# THE GREAT DISCIPLE
## and Other Stories

# The
# Great Disciple
## AND OTHER STORIES

*By* W. B. READY

THE BRUCE PUBLISHING COMPANY
MILWAUKEE

Several of these stories first appeared in the *Atlantic Monthly* and in the *Saturday Evening Post*. Thanks are due to the editors of those journals for their permission to reprint them.

To

NORA HART READY

*The Mother of the Writer*

# CONTENTS

# THE GREAT DISCIPLE

*and Other Stories*

# THE GREAT DISCIPLE

# I

THE Digger Dolan was disgruntled for months over the fact that Dinny Whalen had gone for the priesthood. As soon as he got a few jars inside of him he would be harking back to Dinny's calling. Even in the days of his youth the Digger's face was scarred from the sundry football boots that had scored it, and his bullet head was cropped to the bone, except for a topknot that was like a tonsure in reverse. "Begod," he would say bitterly, slapping the sloppy bar counter with his thick and heavy hand, "begod, as soon as I heard that the Franciscans were after taking Dinny Whalen I was around to the presbytery to see Father Fennell, to offer my services to the Vincentians. And all I got for my pains was a slap in the puss and a boot in the rear from himself; he thought that I had drink taken. Now why should they take Dinny Whalen and leave me a layman? I used to blind Dinny at Catechism." Then the Digger Dolan would glower into his pot before burying his face deep into it.

The whole parish and the whole township, the very county itself was puzzled, like the Digger, over Dinny Whalen's call. The only one who seemed to know all about it was Brother John, and although it wrecked his backfield he it was who must have occasioned the vocation's coming to Dinny. The Whalens, and there were dozens of them, were all good ball players. Nearly every team in the district had a Whalen in it somewhere, but Dinny was the first one ever to get to college, to get the real coaching from Brother John, and of all of us he was the great one. It seems that one year when the Whalens were in the money they sent Dinny to the Brothers for a bit of polish and to wait until there was a job in the steel works for him, along with his brothers and his cousins and the rest of his long-tailed kin. Brother John saw his handling and his running almost right away, and Dinny was brought in among us from that time on. He never left the College for the steel works. Even when times got so bad that the Whalens did not have the fees for him among the whole lot of them, Dinny stayed on. He was, I suppose, Brother John's only football scholarship. Scholar he was certainly. He used to crouch behind us almost as if he were over us, and many times even the opposing team were his puppets. On his day, and he had many such days, he would be conducting the play all over the field, all the time. God be with you, Dinny Whalen. It was given to you, as it is given to few men, to show the glory of being set down, human and knowing, on this earth — and you showed it by playing ball.

None of us were very wealthy, except for Liam Connors, but Dinny Whalen was downright poor. He was so poor that you could smell the tang of poverty upon him, the unwashed sting that the poor can never withhold. It permeates their clothes and their skin, their hair, their breathing even; it is poverty's stigmata. Sometimes some of us, when we were really strapped, would play a few semipro games, and find a rolled Treasury note in the toe of a sock after the game, but Dinny played the semipro games regularly, and it was there that the Digger Dolan again encountered him, as they both played for the money that both of them were needing. The Digger wanted it to augment his meager stipend as a journeyman plasterer, which didn't pay enough for one good night a week, and Dinny needed it to keep himself respectable, not in clothing, but in feeling. He gave his money home, where there were five younger children.

The Digger and Dinny had been in grade school together, and they had been the names that were remembered, among the ruck of Caseys, Dwyers, Nolans, and Sullivans. The Digger was no shoveller at all, but just very wild Irish, and he had been the terror of his class. Even the teachers were afraid of him when he was a beefy baby; and in football games and in street forays the Digger stood pre-eminent. The whole of his adjacent society paid tribute to him, except for Dinny Whalen. Skinny, wiry Dinny could take the Digger apart any time he wanted to, though he never did, for there was no harm in the Digger at all, but just an eager courage and a dull brute strength that was to get him into trouble all his early years. The Digger would charge a pack of hostile forwards with a roar, and go down battling, where Dinny would waltz around them with the jigging swerve of a snipe. As they grew older the Digger became quite the hero in the rough tangles of semipro football, but Dinny would make him look as if he was rooted and not a free agent as he swung an attack against him.

They liked one another, for all their difference. Just before Dinny went for the priesthood he played in the final of the County Cup game against the Digger, and on his performance that day he was awarded the gold medal as the most valuable player in the league. But for him the Digger would have got the medal surely, but whatever he did, there was Dinny ahead of him. It must have been that that sent him, all scarred and beetling, around to see Father Fennell about joining the

Vincentians, because even his most sycophantic followers never could have encouraged the Digger into his quest for sanctity. The Digger did that alone, and it was his last essay, for after that we never saw Dinny more, not for many years, and there was nothing in the area, nor in the adjacent countryside, to trouble the tenor of the Digger Dolan's way.

We went on playing football without Dinny Whalen, and we did well without him. Brother John never seemed to regret his leaving us although in losing him he had lost the one great man that every football coach dreams always of possessing. The years went by, and Dinny Whalen became a memory, and, because he was only just past twenty when he went away, the small world we lived in never really knew him, for it was in the few years later that we really made our fame on the field of play. Sometimes Dinny's father, a humdrum little man, would be out watching us, and we would ask after Dinny, but he would have little news of him, the Franciscans being strict and distant with their novices. There were no annual vacations for Dinny Whalen, the way it was with the boys in the diocesan seminary, being paraded around the houses by their proud mamas, wearing their black suits, and talking about getting minor orders soon. Dinny had been sent out of the country for his training, and his superiors had not even stopped at Italy for his enlightenment, but all the way to China they had sent him, where he was learning the Franciscan way in a distant northern province. We never expected to see him again and, as young men will, we tended to forget him. Besides, for all his quality, he was never really one of us; and with him gone, Brother John, his dream over if ever he had one, was not troubled by his thoughts of Dinny's progress. In a way Brother John seemed glad that he had gone, and, in retrospect, I think we all were glad too.

We never tangled with the Digger Dolan. Sometimes he came out to watch us play, and he always ended by so warmly espousing our cause that the referee would have to stop the game until the uproar caused by the Digger's remarks had quietened down, but he was a local Irishtown character and all of us, however unconsciously, were glad to be in the wider sphere that we had entered through the College. His antics were a frequent cause of conversation among us all, and we pretended to visiting teams that we knew him well, but he was just a character to us, that was all.

Then, just before the war broke out, in the quiet season, between May and August, we all got an engraved card of invitation to the ordination, in the parish church, of the Reverend Malachy Whalen, O.F.M. It was Dinny Whalen, back from China, back to his old parish to be ordained. We had all realized, vaguely, that it was nearly ten years since Dinny had gone away, and for all of that time he had been in China, where the Japanese had been acting up, but that was all we knew, or even thought of knowing. Gradually it began to be known around the parish that Dinny had been in the part of China where the Japanese had been in control, and that he had been very ill, so that his superiors had decided to send him home to recuperate; and, because his ordination was nigh, as a special favor, they had allowed him to be ordained in his own parish. It was very rare for the Franciscans to allow that, they are a very gaunt order, those brown robes. It always has seemed to me that El Greco caught more of the Franciscan spirit than did gentle Giotto.

It was on a Sunday morning, early in June, that the ordination was due to take place. I took my invitation off the dressing table, and, in the sunny quiet morning, called around for Tim McGrath, and we went to church together. We were

well filled with the spacious Sunday feeling, easy and slow,
and we got to the church with about five minutes to spare. We
went in, winked at Justin McCarthy, the constant usher, and
made our way down to the reserved seats, on the right-hand
side. All the team was there, and the Digger Dolan as well.
Brother John sat in the seat ahead of us along with the
Whalens, the whole family of them, who occupied two entire
benches. Behind us the church was full, and in the air was the
scent of fresh roses on the altar over the abiding smell of
stale incense that Joe Hennessey, the thurifer, used to billow
out in such smoking profusion.

We could hear the organ thudding as it began to start up and
then, even on that poor instrument, and with the voices of our
squalling choir, the church came to life as the Archbishop
came down the aisle while the people stood up and knelt down
for his blessing and the building filled with his praise. By the
grace of God and favor of the Apostolic See he was archbishop,
the great priest, who in his days had pleased God. With him
came all the altar servers and the priests. They settled their
flounces and sat down around the altar, and then, from the
Archbishop down to little Timmy Madden, who was the prel-
ate's trainbearer, they looked down the church, and waited for
the coming of the man to be ordained, Dinny Whalen who was,
Father Malachy who was to be.

There was a shuffle and a slapping of sandals down the
aisle, and then he passed our pew, with two of his Franciscan
brethren as attendants. We would never have known him. It
was the greatest shock that I have ever experienced in my life.
Dinny Whalen had been a swank, wiry, jaunty man, with all
his quietude. Now, with his hands crossed in front of him
and with his head bowed low, in the coarse brown habit of the
order, was a thin and emaciated Franciscan, peering carefully

at the ground ahead of him through steel-rimmed spectacles. A sparse black beard covered his jaws and chin, and his neck stood out scrawny from his cowl. His nose had been broken and twisted, and his curly black hair lay dank and spare around his skullcap. It was Dinny Whalen all right, but the change that had come over him was almost beyond all bearing. I looked up and saw his mother's face, as she looked at this aging monk, who had been her lovely boy, and the tears were running down her face. Brother John had put his arm under hers, and he too was looking intently at the three Franciscans as they passed up to the altar. The Digger Dolan looked around at us wildly, to see if we thought as he did, and then we sank on our knees, while they vested the fragile neophyte.

The ceremony went its traditional and ceremonious way, but none of us were following our missals. We were looking at the stooped figure of our onetime comrade, who, near as he was, seemed further away from us than if we had never known him. The sermon was preached by one of the Franciscans, a burly Chinaman with a fluting foreign voice.

Gradually the time came, and the Archbishop laid his hands upon him, and Dinny Whalen became Father Malachy forevermore. As the celebration finished, the new priest came down to the benches, and blessed his mother and his father. Then he turned to Brother John, and blessed him, and lifted him up, and, with a gap-toothed grin, put his arms around him in a fraternal embrace. The two of them stood there looking at one another for about a minute, and they were both so satisfied with one another that it seemed as if they were alone, as they really were. They were somewhere we shall never know.

The new priest, with his battered face and his broken teeth, then blessed the whole two rows of football players who had come to see him and who were only now seeing him. He sought for the Digger Dolan, and leaning over us, in his starched white alb and dangling maniple he said,

"Here Digger, this is yours. You always did deserve it. God bless you, boy." And with that he gave to Digger the gold medal that he had won, so many years before, for being the best player in the league, over the head of the Digger Dolan.

Then the whole church gathered around him, and he was lost to us. I never saw him again. Soon after that he went back to the Far East and was there all through the late great war. The last I heard of him he was a prior in a Franciscan settlement in the Holy Land.

It is no wonder to me now why Brother John did not mind his leaving us early. He was the only one of us who knew what Brother John was meaning. He even knew better than Brother John.

# II

## ST. PATRICK'S DAY IN THE AFTERNOON

ALL for tripping a wing, Scrammy Ryan had to leave his native land and flee to Iowa, where he is as safe as he can be from the wrath of the men of Coonakilty. Scrammy is an old man now, a dignified, shy, retiring little bit of a man, and to look at him nobody would ever know that he is entering the legend of Ireland, where his fame will be as secure in West Cork as that of Finn MacCool or Sean Tracy. The children of his native township of Barryowen learn of his great exploit from the old people, as they sit wide eyed around the glowing turf fire of an evening, listening as they hear tell of Cuchulain, the Hound of Ulster, of Red Hugh O'Donnell, who is buried in Spain, and of Grania of the shining bosom, the snowy-breasted pearl. Scrammy, still living, is talked of along with these long-dead creatures. In Coonakilty, too, his name is often mentioned, and is included in the curses of the old crones, along with the names of Oliver Cromwell and David Lloyd George, which is a high measure of fame indeed for a man who runs the elevator in the only hotel in a little Midwest town.

As the children who are hearing the story now will grow up and scatter, leaving their homely places, as most young Irish do, to seek fame and fortune in the green fields of America, they will bring the story with them, and their children's children will pass it on to a Western world, so that Scrammy's fame may even penetrate into Iowa in the years to come. The elevator which he pilots up and down, these days, may even have a panel inscribed to him in some future year: *Scrammy Ryan found a refuge here, after tripping the wing of Coonakilty.* He might even attain the distinction of having a brand of whisky named after him, and the Dublin Players might even include a play about him in their repertoire, in blank verse, along with their plays of Cathleen ni Houlihan and the Croppy Boy.

Scrammy's fame is secure, but because the years may distort the story it is well to recount it now, before the Barryowen people glorify it too much or the Coonakilty folk, by their vituperation, turn it into a lampoon.

Until that day, that fateful day, March 17, 1903, Scrammy was just one of the lads of the village. He would never be noticed in a crowd of more than three. There was nothing about him to show the glory that was impending, the glory that was to be his before that day was done. The great day started quietly. The Coonakilty team, with their supporters, arrived about eleven in the morning, and while the supporters started to belt the bottle, the playing men swaggered down the main street, flexing their muscles, laughing scornfully with one another over the idea that these Barryowen jackeens could constitute a threat to their supremacy.

Every year the four townships of Barryowen, Coonakilty, Ballygunnion, and Slievduddy played one another at football. If any team managed to beat the other three teams, it was awarded the Triple Crown, a wonderful award that didn't exist in actuality, but was an imaginary trophy that was very rarely won. So keen was the competition that when Coonakilty had played Slievduddy on the previous Boxing Day, and the football had been torn to pieces, neither team paused at all, but went right on with the game with flying fists, until Con Leary had time from his shouting to blow up another one.

The game between Coonakilty and Barryowen was the last of the series. Both teams had beaten the other two. The Triple Crown was to be won by one of them upon that St. Patrick's Day, and there was a deep undercurrent of excitement throughout West Cork as to which team was going to be victorious. So intense was the excitement that the *Skibbereen Eagle* had sent a special correspondent down to report upon the struggle, and had supplied him with carrier pigeons so that he could air-mail his dispatch to the waiting metropolis.

The game that these townships played bore a cursory and superficial resemblance to Rugby football. There were fifteen men on either side, and they could pick up the ball and run with it, but it was only the boldest of men that would venture to do so. The four townships had introduced variations of their own into the game. The only thing that was really frowned upon was to use some artificial implement, other than the boot or the heavy brass rings, with which to induce an opponent to give ground. The ball spent most of the ninety minutes of play in the midst of the thirty players who fought in close formation to get to one end of the field or the other, and when they had reached it they would fall exhausted on the ball until their supporters could intimidate the referee into admitting that they had crossed their opponents' line.

The football teams were the heroes of their parishes and townships. As might be expected, they were picked more for their battling quality in solid slugging than for their dexterity in handling a ball. Sometimes a team would include a footrunner, who would shiver on the wing except for once or twice in a game, when a bullet-headed and scarred coplayer would sneak out of the melee with the ball hidden under his jersey and pass it to the fleet one, who would then run for the opponents' line like the hammers of hell, with the whole fifteen of the opposition giving tongue and chasing him when they discovered how they had been deceived. The fury of his pursuers so unnerved Tommy Mulcahy a few years previously that he didn't stop when he got to the goal line, but ran straight on with the ball under his arm until he dropped panting in his mother's cabin in Loughnabreda, four miles away.

The game had developed over the centuries and the Church had begun to make it Christian by dropping a ball amid the battling heroes. It was very rarely that men died as a result of the games, but there were always a few punchies around the district who were treated with the consideration that is given to the afflicted by a God-fearing people, especially when the affliction is the result of fighting the good fight.

Scrammy was strictly a supporter, and he was never too vociferous a one. One could never tell if one were standing by friend or foe, and some of the other township supporters would as soon brain a rival with an empty bottle as look at him. Indeed, Scrammy's brother Jim had been a little queer ever since he shouted "Up Barryowen!" at the wrong time and in the wrong place five years previously. Not that there was really anything the matter with Jim, except that he shouted "Up Barryowen!" all the time since, and seemed to have forgotten all the other fine conversational phrases that he used to have. So Scrammy was always a wee bit cautious before he let loose with his encouragement. It seems that all the great heroic deeds come from men like Scrammy, who up to the very deed never seem to have nerve enough to say "Boo!" to a goose.

By three o'clock in the afternoon the town of Barryowen

was filled to overflowing. The beer shops in O'Connell Street were jammed to the doors, and foaming pints of porter were passed out over the heads of people to the crowds standing in the streets. All the adjacent townships had come into Barry-owen for the game, forsaking their own Paddy's Day celebrations in order to see the bloody murder that was due to start at half-past three on the Parish Field, behind Township School.

The old priest, Father Mullins, God rest his soul, would never let the game be played there, because it was hallowed ground, but the new priest, God bless him, never tried to stop them. He told the organizers to go right ahead, only they had to charge a shilling a head to cover the expenses, and pass the plate around at half time for the Church Building Fund.

Just before the game was due to start, there was a crowd of about ten thousand people gathered around the pitch. Parky Cleary had got a tent up, and had the concession to sell porter on the field. The Sons of Erin fife and drum band screamed away at one end of the field, while the Hibernian pipers marched up and down the pitch playing strictly impartial tunes like "Soul of My Saviour" and "The Canadian Boat Song." The bookmakers had their stands up, and were shouting the odds, which were seven to five on Barryowen, it being their home ground.

Behind the hedge there was a bit of cockfighting going on, and Owen Downey, with drink taken, was offering to fight any man in West Cork for a stake of five pounds, there and then. The local constabulary had decided to take in a convention at Cork for that day — it were better so; and the military had a flying squad sitting in the wagons at the barracks just in case the natural excitement of the day should start off an uprising. It was a lovely day — the weather was tailored for the occasion.

The two teams shouldered their way through the crowd and onto the field. The Coonakilty team had used the Dolphin Hotel for their changing quarters, while Barryowen had changed in the humbler Mooney's Bar. While the home team wore their well-known saffron jerseys, with the green shamrocks over the hearts, Coonakilty had come out with a glorious new regalia of clean jerseys hooped in orange, white, and green. They even had numbers on the back of them. There was not much to choose between the teams as they stood glowering at one another while poor Mr. O'Neil, the referee, kept them waiting while he got back another large whisky at the rear of Parky Cleary's tent to keep his courage up. The air was tense; silence had descended on the crowd as they waited for the whistle to blow.

Mr. O'Neil blew a faltering blast, and with a scream Spike Leahy kicked off for Coonakilty. A foolhardy Barryowen forward tried to gather the ball. Before he could get it away from himself the enemy was on him howling, and the issue was joined. The thud could be heard for acres as the two teams crashed into each other. The mothers praying in their cabins flinched, and the fathers licked their lips and swallowed dry. Both teams were locked in a flailing combat, except for a little foot-runner whom Coonakilty had brought with them in case there was a chance of a stealthy run.

The crowd was so packed that they were standing right upon the lines of the field of play. Scrammy himself, jammed among his own supporters — he had seen to that — was hovering on the touchline. Within a quarter of an hour it became evident to everyone that this game was to be the battle of the century.

The teams swayed back and fore across the field; up and down they fought their way, with the ball in the middle of them, never quite making either end of the field. The soft Irish turf became as churned up as a farmyard midden, and the teams were almost unrecognizable from one another, so covered were they with mud and blood and spittle, with their jerseys torn, their hair all matted, and their grunts and their staring eyes, their bruised faces, and their sagging bodies making them all appear alike except to the initiated.

When the first half of the game was over, and the battlers sucked their lemons and were wiped off by the bucket boys, the spectators looked at one another and shook their heads in silent delight. This was a game for the record. It was a memorable occasion and the crowd realized it, not even leaving their places at half time to go to Cleary's, lest they miss one precious minute of the second half. While this Homeric struggle was proceeding their womenfolk were shopping downtown, for this was strictly a man's spectacle, but the women cast many an uneasy glance up to Parish Field, for the great noise and the even greater silence told them that great things were portending.

The second half began with a rush and a roar. The brief interval had worked wonders for the team, and the battle went on as ferociously as ever. Scrammy was sweating with excitement by this time, and had even essayed a timid howl when he knew that it would be smothered in an enveloping roar from the crowd. The little foot-runner from Coonakilty was so hopping with excitement that he had actually tried to get into the fray, only to come whizzing out of it like a cork from a bottle when he did try.

It seemed as if men could not keep up the pace so long, but the battle, now become silent and dour, went on and on, with no score, until only ten minutes were left for play. Then, when the Barryowen team were battling right on the enemy's goal line, Spike Leahy, the Coonakilty captain, staggered out of the scrum with the ball under his oxter and lobbed it to the little foot-runner, who hared up the field with it.

There was a stunned moment of silence before the crowd roared out a warning to the Barryowen team, who looked up from their pummeling to find that their fleet fresh enemy was nearly halfway up the field and going like a steam engine. With a bellow the Barryowen team started after him like a stamping herd, but it was hopeless from the start. So confident was the Coonakilty pedestrian that he slowed down to a gallop, and even took time off to look behind him, and therein was his undoing, for as he did so Scrammy Ryan put his foot out and tripped him.

Scrammy Ryan, the mouse of Barryowen, put his foot out and tripped the foot-runner, in full view of the field.

Mr. O'Neil blew a blast on his whistle, a silence descended, except for the gasping of the pedestrian, and the full magnitude of the occasion burst on Scrammy and on the Coonakilty men at the same time. With a terrified lunge Scrammy pushed back through the crowd as at the same moment seven of the Coonakilty forwards began to tear their way through the spectators to get him. They threw grown men over their shoulders, so eager were they to get their hands and feet on Scrammy. The crowd remained passive. The situation was too big for it. Then, as Scrammy broke clear of the crowd the Coonakilty pack gave tongue. They were clear too, and Scrammy was only about fifty yards nearer the gate than they were.

Fear gave Scrammy wings. Some say he went so quickly past them that the wind ruffled their clothes. Anyway, he was halfway down O'Connell Street before the seven Coonakilty avengers, all torn and bloodied in their football rig, came storming out of the gate behind him, leaving in their wake an

awe-struck crowd, a depleted Coonakilty team all jibbering
with rage, an apprehensive referee, and a cool and grinning
team of Barryowen.

Fleur Driscoll, the Barryowen captain, was a crafty, foxy,
red-haired man. He went up to the nonplused O'Neil, the
referee, and insisted that the game go on. Dusk was falling,
the protests of Spike Leahy and the remainder of the Coonakilty team were of no avail, and the game went on. Spike did
nothing with his penalty kick, and Barryowen began to cross
the Coonakilty line at will. They scored sixty points before
the final whistle blew. Coonakilty staggered off the field broken
men. They looked wildly around, hoping to God that their
supporters would start something, but they seemed far away,
straining, listening, with the rest of the silent crowd.

Players and spectators all stayed silent, listening. Then,
from afar off, came a thin scream, from beyond O'Connell
Street. It sounded something like the noise a rabbit makes
when it is caught by a badger. But they all knew that this was
no rabbit scream, but the voice of Scrammy Ryan in his
agony as he turned at bay outside the Emporium window.
Then there was a crash of glass, and silence. All the men slowly
took off their hats, and the teams slowly wended their way to
their changing quarters.

There was no celebration in Barryowen that night. The
Coonakilty men and the men from the other townships went
away, and left Barryowen to its grief. Barryowen had won the
Triple Crown, but Scrammy was a bitter price to pay for it.
"Holy God," said Driscoll, emotionally, as the team quaffed
their porter mournfully in Mooney's. "Holy God, if it was
one of us it wouldn't matter at all, but that poor wee mouse
Scrammy. He must have loved Barryowen."

They dragged the river, but they couldn't find Scrammy's

corpse, and Father Muldoon, despite their pleading, refused to have a funeral without one. The town felt cheated of these last rites, so they had a grand concert, with the proceeds of which they hoped to provide for poor Jim Ryan, who was left bereft, now that Scrammy had gone. Jim's "Up Barryowen!" had become more constant since Scrammy had passed away, and the mournful sound of it was like a knell to the people of Barryowen.

A special meeting of the Four Townships' Football Club was held, and a letter was read from the Bishop condemning the plays and forbidding them in future. Actually the Bishop was delighted with the opportunity to put a ban on the pagan festival, but his letter included a prayer for poor Scrammy, and roundly castigated the Coonakilty men, to the open joy of the other three townships.

Then, when it seemed to be all over, and Barryowen was left as perpetual owner of the Triple Crown, a public subscription was opened in Barryowen, and an actual triple crown was bought, something like the Pope's hat, and on it was inscribed: *The Triple Crown, won by Barryowen in perpetuity, from all comers.* Coonakilty was in disgrace, and Barryowen was riding high. All their triumph was put in jeopardy, however, by a postcard that Fleur Driscoll got at the post office. It was a colored card of the City of Cork, and scrawled on it was "I'm here. S.R." Fleur Driscoll swore quietly, then grinned, and closing the post office went around to tell the rest of the town.

The news had to be kept quiet, because Coonakilty, to stop the Bishop's nattering, was on the point of putting up a stained-glass window to Scrammy in the procathedral hall. In spite of the pledges to secrecy that he obtained, all Barryowen had Fleur Driscoll's news before the day was out. Father Muldoon, a Barryowen boy himself, and the bank manager drew out Scrammy's savings from the bank and gave the whole £85 of it to Fleur with instructions to buy Scrammy a ticket, an £85 ticket, and told him to get Scrammy on the next boat sailing out of Cork, east or west, as long as it was going far. That's how Scrammy came to Iowa.

The Coonakilty men didn't get the news until the window was erected "by the sorrowing citizens of Coonakilty," and they couldn't convince the Bishop of the story. The people of Barryowen and Ballygunnion and Slievduddy just rocked with delight when they heard the story of Scrammy's scrambling out of the river, all cut with glass, and bruised and wet, and how he sneaked out of town in terror. It didn't make his feat any the less memorable, and it made even greater fools out of Coonakilty.

In Barryowen simple old Jim Ryan still calls out "Up Barryowen!" and the Coonakilty people wince when they hear it still; and in Iowa, in the Middle West, Scrammy pilots his purring craft up and down, and remembers his great day, the excitement, the impulse, the terror, and the glory of it.

# III

## BARRING THE WEIGHT

I THINK that the only deep sorrow that Brother John ever had was that we were a pack of small forwards. There were always God's plenty of big powerful backs, but his forwards never ran to much more than 150-pounders, which was just damned silly in a league where we were up against teams with lumbering heavy packs. We puzzled over it, but there was nothing we could do about it. Dinny Sullivan was a fine heavy man, but he was so lithe and dexterous and cunning that it was a sin not to make a three-quarter out of him, and Eddie Walsh was as wide as a door, but he was such a graceful swerving runner that to put him in the pack was to yoke a thoroughbred with a mule team.

It wasn't just one season; year after year the same thing happened. The forwards were built like the backs, and the backs were big enough to be forwards. I remember Brother John's eyes lighting up when Jack Cotter came to us from one of the North Country colleges. He was a fine figure of a man, well over six feet in height and weighing about 210 pounds. A second-row forward, he was proud and happy in that position. He nearly killed us packing down with him, but at last we were getting the ball in the tight scrums, and the backs were getting a chance to throw it around.

But it didn't last long. Cotter was a good forward, but

Brother John saw him fooling around after practice one night, and he saw that the big fellow could really kick and field a ball. He made him into J. Cotter, the great All-Ireland full-back, but he still wanted his fine big bustling pack instead of the sharp little terriers he had in the likes of me. After a game, as we would limp off the field, bruised and battered by bigger men, we would wish almost savagely that we were huskier, because a burly pack was all that Brother John needed to win the All-Ireland championship.

He was the greatest coach I have ever seen, and he never had to raise his voice. I can see him now, although he's been under the sod these few years, God rest him. He was tall and gray, and stooped. He could only have been a schoolmaster, and even during the holidays there was always a dusting of chalk around him. His face was so Irish that it had a Spanish look, and his thick gray hair grew back from his forehead in the same sort of pompadour as did Jim Corbett's, the fighter. He was vice-principal of the school, and his gentle air fooled nobody. There was iron in the man, and sometimes bitterness would break out of him, so that the Principal and the Provincial and even the Bishop were wary of him. He was a hidden sort of man, and there are plenty of them in Ireland. History was his subject, but Rugby football was his delight. It was far more than a game to him: the strife and the checks, the teamwork and the play, were life as it should be to Brother John.

We'd nearly choke with temper as game after game we would be pushed off the ball by big agricultural louts with no more science than one of those bulldozers they are using now. In the dressing rooms after the game, Brother John would compliment us in his soft Kerry voice: "You played the grand game, Willie. . . . That was a grand tackle of yours, Con. . . . The big fellow never laid a finger on you, Terry. . . ." And all the time we would be glum, drying ourselves silently after the showers. Mick Yewlett, the trainer, would look up from the massage board, where he'd be rubbing one of us: "Ah, Brother, if we had the weight, these boys would beat the world; be God they'd even give Presentation College a run for it!"

But Brother John would never murmur against our flimsiness. "It's the will of God, Michael," was all he would say. But all the days of his life he'd wanted to train the All-Ireland team, and we'd have been a team of champions, barring the weight. I was a member of that team, but I must see a better team before I yield to it. The way we got that ball back from a loose maul I've not seen equaled since. We had the heart, the almost functional perfection of a good machine. We had everything, barring the weight. We'd have gladly changed ourselves into big blond Saxons for the season if it would have brought Brother John the championship.

We were all in our last year in school, and had been playing together for five or six years. We were far out of the class of the average local team, and most of our opponents were university or town teams, but we had to struggle desperately to beat these lesser men, because they had the weight. After twelve games we were still the invincibles, but it was a struggle all the time. For us forwards it was our last season; we'd never make the weight for a university or town team, so that season had all the sweetness of a golden era departing.

Our football field was beside a ruined castle, and in the soft Irish evenings, when the quiet of Christ would be on everything, the thud of boot on ball and the grunts of the tackles would carry clear across to the pavilion where some of us would be sitting around Brother John as he explained some play. The plays he designed were to him not only for the football field, but contained his ideas about everything. He had been brought up on the old nineteenth-century nationalism, and he saw us as a bunch of Cuchulainns, small dark sad men, who would go down in glory before inevitable circumstance. I can see that now, though of course I didn't then.

As the games went on, a faint, dim gleam of hope began to flicker. We were the only undefeated team in the county, then in the province. There were good days and bad days, but we always managed to win, sometimes more by the grace of God than by anything else. And then Abertaff asked us for a game! They had beaten the Australian touring team; they had more internationals playing for them than any other team in Wales. Indeed it was almost as much of an honor to play for them as to play for Wales. They had an Irish tour every year, and apparently they had decided that they needed a preliminary loosener before tangling up with the tough opposition that led them such a dance every year. So they had picked a school team, and we were the team. We began to train with an intensity that worried Brother John; it was the only chance we would ever have against a first-class side and we knew it. Abertaff would surely beat us, but by God they'd play Rugby to beat us!

We played them on the Castle Ground. I remember it was in late February, the second Saturday in Lent. There was a great crowd out to see the game, the biggest crowd any of us had ever played before. The Abertaff pack were big burly men, steelworkers, County Constabulary, dockers, and the like. They were led by the great Lem Jenkins, who had led the Welsh pack for the past two seasons. He was a big bull of a man, and as I left my father, God rest his soul, to run on the field, he took another look at Lem and said to me, "He'll kill you, my son. I'm glad your mother stayed home."

Lem was my opposite number; he gave me a friendly nod, which I tried to return nonchalantly, but I had to chew my gum very hard to get any moisture in my mouth, although the palms of my hands were wet with sweat. Brother John was away in a corner of the field shaking. He thought he was sending us to glory, and it before our time, and we did look a puny pack beside that solid Welsh forward line. Also their famous red and black jerseys were clean and new, their ringed stockings matched, and they were wearing swagger ballooned shorts, so that we looked tawdry as well as scrawny beside them.

I saw Brother Principal grimacing as he compared us, and I knew that Brother John was in for another rollicking there, besides the complaints from our parents, who were already ganging up on him as they saw the logical result of the clash between Abertaff and ourselves. They knew that we were out for glory, and that because we could not bring him the championship we were going to be his small dark heroes who would solace him by dour struggle in a hopeless cause.

The whistle blew, and Eddie Walsh kicked off. Before the Abertaff man could gather it to find touch we were on him, the whole forward line. We swarmed all over him, and went on with the ball in a forward rush, only to be recalled for being off side. That was the game throughout. Abertaff was out for the exercise, and we were out for Brother John. They held us off good-humoredly at first, but gradually our panting silent tenseness communicated itself to them, and they began to play football with all their national genius.

At half time there was nothing in it, no score in the hardest game either team had ever played. It wasn't the finest game, only the hardest, because in a fine game there is often a sort of careless rapture, when one time or another the unusual or bizarre play is tried. But nobody was taking any chances in this game. The orthodox passing movements would start cautiously and be smothered by furious tackling. Abertaff got the ball from every set scrum, and we got it from most of the loose mauls. The crowd was so excited that there seemed to be a blurred roar all the time, but I never had time to look at them.

At half time Mick Yewlett ran on the field with his inevitable sponge and bucket of water, and rubbed our faces clear of mud and spittle. Brother John was among us, murmuring, "Boys. . . . Oh, boys." I remember that we just grinned at him, and didn't say anything. Somehow all of us felt more grown up than we had ever felt before. It was evident to all of us that his coaching was paying off. Our lightness and speed were useless in the set scrums, so we were giving them to the Welshmen, and we were running them off their feet all over the field.

But in the second half the inevitable began to run us down. Our legs began to weaken. We couldn't push all that Welsh weight around without beginning to feel it. And we were as bruised as we could be without breaking off, yet somehow we still managed to get there in time, until at last their Dai Evans got off on a clear run. Nobody ever caught Dai once he was away; he scored a try, and Gruffydd converted it for them. So they got five points, but no more, and Lem Jenkins was out of the game for weeks with a twisted knee. The final whistle went on two exhausted teams. The crowd was delighted with us, and friends crowded around us. But we pushed our limping way through them and gathered around Brother John. We didn't say a word, and neither did he, but he knew, and we knew, that in our defeat we had won something greater than a championship.

We never were any good for the rest of the season; we played almost as dreamily as Brother John now coached us.

The championship receded from our minds; we never really woke up on the field after that second Saturday in Lent. Abertaff never played us again; they explained that we were not quite what they were looking for. Mind you, we never expected to play them again. That once was enough to give us our experience, and to give Brother John the great occasion. We were on our way out, it was our last year in school.

There's a photograph of the team hanging up over there behind the davenport, contagious to that aquatint of Galway Bay. The wee fellow holding the ball was the pack leader, and that's Brother John sitting beside him. There's myself, I'm heavier now, and alongside me is Tim Coghlan; he was killed, God rest him, at Anzio. All the small fellows are sitting down, and they are all the forwards. The man adjacent to Tim is Con Daly. Do you notice the grin on him? He was always bemoaning his bad luck, and he always ended with ". . . and to cap it all I'll probably marry a fruitful wife!" Our hooker used to ask Con, savagely and blasphemously, to push harder, and back would come Coneen, "Tom, Tom, me navel's scarring the ground." And so it went.

Brother John was retired the next year to the Brothers' House at Waterford, and he died there early in 1940. The team was the right age for the war. Nine of them were killed, including poor Con. God rest them all. My memories of happier days are all tied up with them, and the great team we were, barring the weight.

# IV

## "SUFFICIENT"

EVAN MORGAN was the Valley's star. He was the pride of Wales, the envy of England, and the wonder of the world. Never since Ianto Fullpelt had first pulled on his kicking boots had a ballplayer been seen like Evan Morgan. Evan Morgan was only his proper name. Because of the outward curving arch of his bowed and powerful legs he was known to all the Welshmen as Evans Bandy. There was no English about him at all. When he was not practicing his vocation as a ballplayer he used to work as a collier in the coal mine of Pontllanfrw, which was near his home in the village of Bwllhelli, where he lived with his widowed mother.

Evans Bandy never gave a sign that he knew of the glory that was his. He was a quiet, decent fellow, strictly an amateur in the football game, and there was no side about him whatever. He would turn up at Cardiff railway station on his way to play against England at London, and all his belongings would be wrapped up in a neatly tied paper parcel. He never wore a collar or tie, but the clean soft muffler that, together with the cloth cap, were the mark of the collier off duty. He would never be noticed in a crowd, but on the football field he assumed a power that was unmistakable. Up in Edinburgh, in Scotland, Evan would recover the ball and get it safely into touch before the Scots could lay a finger on him, and in Dublin, Ireland,

27

he frequently dictated the game to the Irish pack. The Welsh-men watching him would set up a paean of praise at his manipulations.

"There he is for you!" they would say, triumphantly point-ing out Evan to the other nation. "There he is, our lovely boy. Greatest since Fullpelt he is, for sure. Come on, Evans, bachan. Come on, my lovely boys, give the ball to Bandy. Raised in the green pastures of football he was, the Rhondda Valley!"

Evan was the darling of his country when the football season was on. Year after year he played for Wales, in front of tens of thousands of people, but it never bothered him. Straight after the match, back he would go to Bwllhelli, to his mother's cottage, and on Monday mornings he would start back at the colliery as if the previous Saturday he had not been the cynosure of scores of thousands of eyes. It would be thought, in the Rhondda Valley, that that would be enough of a life for any man, but Evans Bandy, in spite of it, remained a discon-tented man, and all because of Gwenllian Nest Jenkins.

Nearly any girl in the Rhondda would have liked to have Evan courting her, but not Gwenllian Nest. Since she had started going to Cardiff College there had been no holding her, and Jenkins the Bank, her father, used to bemoan the change that had come over his daughter to the other deacons at chapel meetings. Nothing would do that Gwenllian girl now, if you please, but that they speak English in the house. She had become English mad since they had sent her to that old Cardiff College, instead of to Llandudno, where her mother had gone.

"Diu! would you believe it," said Evans the Shop, "that a girl like Gwenllian should be so unnatural? There is a lovely girl she was growing up too, look you. A blessing it is that Mrs. Jenkins has passed away."

That was not all. On top of all that she had begun bringing her boy friend home from Cardiff for the week ends. Not only was he not chapel, but he couldn't speak Welsh, and although he played Rugby football for college he would not play for Wales, when he was chosen, but said that he would wait until England claimed him, as he was more English than Welsh. He was a fine stocky lump of an outside-half, and maybe he was being cunning when he refused Wales, because he was only invited when Evans Bandy was recovering from a fractured limb or from a torn body, and the cunning fellow, indeed he did not have to be very cunning, would know that he was only a substitute for a greater man. Still, to the Valley Welsh there was something very suspect, naturally, in a man that would prefer to play for England, even steadily, when there was even a chance of a single game for Wales.

Evans Bandy had never been much of a man for women when he was growing up. He was too filled with his mission as a ballplayer, and the men of the vale would have smothered any diversion that might have interfered with his development. Now, however, that he had become the whole man, the nonpareil, there was time for dalliance, and even marriage, as long as he did not overdo it, and Evans Bandy looked toward Gwenllian Nest Jenkins. He had looked at her shyly when he was in the village school with her, he, the only son of a father who had been killed in the Senghennydd disaster, being brought up meagerly by his mother on the compensation pittance, and Gwenllian the daughter of Jenkins the Bank. They had gone to the same chapel, naturally, but no more than that at any time. Nevertheless Gwenllian Nest had been noticing him, although she had never shown him so. Now, however, he was Evans Bandy, and in the Rhondda Valley, in the halls of Cardiff College, in Llantarnam Castle itself he was the man of his time. Principal Sir Dilwyn Jones, himself, and Lord Glamorgan used to publicly laud the plays of Evans Bandy, and to any girl it would have been a signal honor to be courted by him. Not exactly any girl, but any Welsh girl; but Gwenllian had begun to go all English, studying that old Shakespeare instead of Gwylym Fawr, the great Welsh playwright. Shakespeare was good, look you, but better in Welsh than in English. That was bad enough, but on top of it she had begun to turn up her nose at the valleys and the coal tips of Wales and had begun to yearn for a job in London when she graduated, although what in the name of Heaven London could offer that could not be found in the metropolis of Cardiff was beyond the Rhondda folk when they heard of her ambition. Her young swain urged her on in these thoughts. In a year he would be able to get a job out of "provincial" Wales, and, playing for a London football club, and with Gwenllian Nest on his arm, there was nothing that he could think of better.

Some of the Valley folk thought that Evans Bandy would be well rid of his inamorata, as the Reverend Davies called Gwenllian, but Evan did not think so, and when he began to brood on it, and the Scots game only six weeks hence, the people changed their opinions as well. A deputation of local notables called on Gwenllian one week end, thinking the girl could not appreciate the situation, but Gwenllian just tossed her head at them with its fair and curly hair, and went right on with her course, which was likely to destroy the hopes of Wales and set Scotland piping in triumph. Everybody despaired of Gwenllian, except Evans Bandy. He had begun to work things out, sweating in the black and gleaming mine shafts.

It took him a long time to work things out, especially as he did all his thinking in Welsh, but at last he made a plan, and once a plan was formed in Evans Bandy's mind not all the weight of an Irish pack could haze him.

Weeks went by. Evan remained the pale and hopeless lover, but there were no sighs out of him. He even practiced football on the chapel field every evening, while from the open windows of Zion the congregation watched him while they sang "Cwm Rhondda," "Sospan Fach," and "Jesu Lover of My Soul" in preparation for the coming international encounter with Scotland. From all over the Valley the boys would come to help Evans Bandy prepare for football. Young men would drive maddened cattle at him, to simulate an Irish forward rush, they would push wagons against him to resemble the steady relentless drive of the English forwards, and the bigger and better of them would come screaming at him like Highlanders, so that he could quench their slogans. Evan did his practices solidly, but the craft, so like that of Ulysses, seemed to absent itself from him; still he was fit. All he lacked was the fire, and he was determined to get that before the game was due.

On Friday evening, and the game was on the following day, in Cardiff, against Scotland, Evan Morgan, properly dressed, called at the house of Jenkins the Bank. Gwenllian answered the door, and her young man was standing beyond her, back in the hallway.

"Nos dda, Gwenllian. . . ." That was as far as Evan could get before the swank young college lad broke in:

"Speak English, can't you?" He said it insolently, confident in his strength and in his dexterity, for while Evan was just a ballplayer, he, Jim Reynolds, was a famous middleweight fighting man, besides being a ballplayer, and a bright future had been forecast for him should he ever consider going professional.

"Speak English, can't you — Taffy?" He said it again, and added "Taffy," which, as everybody knows, is the worst insult one can give a Welshman. And he stood there, behind Gwenllian, smiling and flexing his muscles, driving one coiled fist into the cup of the other hand.

"Gwenllian I was speaking to," said Evan slowly, correctly, as one who did not have much English about him. "Gwenllian I will speak to in her own language." And Evan spoke volubly yet steadily to his beloved.

As he spoke, her eyes widened and her hand went to her throat, but she was pleased, that was obvious, for, being a woman, what Evan was saying to her was a delight.

Gwenllian turned around and said to Jim Reynolds, a little breathlessly, in English:

"Evan here wants to fight you for me. Here, on the mountainside, now. In the Valley there has always been this way of deciding who a girl will marry, if she has more suitors than one, and they are proper men."

Jim Reynolds should have known from that moment, as the reader is bound to know, being perspicacious, that he had lost Gwenllian from that time, but the big lout grinned rather cruelly, and said:

"Now, Taffy? Do you want to fight now? It's the big game tomorrow." At that, a smile of delight came over his face, for if he fought Evans Bandy now, and hurt him sufficiently, so that he could never play football again, why then, he would play for Wales, and that securely, knowing that he could never be replaced by Evan, and Reynolds, being a fighter, which Evan was not, knew plenty of ways to hurt a man so that he stayed hurt.

He pushed past Gwenllian, and taking Evan by the arm, as cordially as he knew how, almost pulled him up to the mountainside, where a little group of men were waiting. This mountain fighting was by no means a vulgar public spectacle. Just a few referees and a doctor and a parson, that was all, and Evans Bandy had them briefed and waiting. The whole population, according to custom, herded their children indoors and themselves shut their eyes and ears to the contest, waiting for the victor to stagger down the high street as a sign that it was over.

"Young men," said the Reverend, slowly and in English, for the sake of Reynolds, "you do know what you are fighting for. Remember that it is bare-fist fighting, with no holds barred. A man is allowed a minute after each knockdown or throw, and the first man to shout 'sufficient' is the loser. Is that clear?"

The two men nodded, stripped down to the upper buff and went at it. Evan Morgan suddenly looked like Evans Bandy, crouching low down, his arms hanging loose, waiting to get his hands on Jim Reynolds, who had a beautiful shuffling stance, whose left shot out like a piston, whose right came over like a hammer, and in no time at all the short, springy, nibbled grass was red with Bandy's blood. Occasionally Bandy would bore in and crash Reynolds to earth, shaking the wind out of him. Occasionally he would sledge-hammer a blow to Reynolds' body, but Bandy was being cut to pieces, coolly, scientifically. He was a beaten man, according to all the canons of fighting. But after every knockdown blow, even when his right eye had to be opened by hand, he would come back, boring in. Reynolds hit him with everything he had, until his breath was coming tearing out of him, and still came Evans Bandy. At last, the crafty wary Evan saw his chance. He got his shoulder in Reynolds' stomach, as if he was going to tackle him, and then he strained on his bowed and powerful legs, and lifted his rival clean off the ground. He got his hands on the thighs of his opponent and, with a mighty heaving grunt, he almost pushed him straight up in the air. Whirling and staggering he threw him away from him, and a moment later, before Reynolds could really hit the friendly ground, he brought his elbow around so that it caught the staggering one under the chin and hit him upright; at the same time he brought his knee up so that the falling face was met by it, and the fight was over, with the broken Reynolds muttering, "Sufficient! Sufficient!"

"Diu! Was that the word?" said Evan in Welsh to those who stood around. "Was that the word? I've been trying to think of that word for the past ten minutes." But nobody will ever know whether he meant that or not.

Down the village high street Evan staggered, with his hands and his boots and his body covered red. He stopped in front of the house of Jenkins the Bank, just looking, and went on home.

Next day, discolored, bruised, and battered, he pulled on the scarlet jersey of the Welsh team, and on to the field he went, to play his great game. He kicked a bit more than usual, but with the wind, which was the best thing to do anyway, and he won the game for Wales with his passing.

Many more games did Evan Morgan play for Wales. A supervisor he did become at the colliery, and Gwenllian Nest married him, as she now says to herself she meant to all the time. They speak Welsh in the house always, so that Evan never has to bother about that old word "sufficient," and they have fine children, six of them, God bless them.

# V

# ANGHARAD

ANGHARAD her name was, although until the day that she heard Matthew Hart say Angharad she had all the time wished that it wasn't. Through school and college, through graduate nursing, her name had been an old nuisance to her. It was a lovely name, for sure, when her mama or her dada said it, but it needed the Welsh tongue to get around it, and outside of home it sounded odd, like Anggie, until Matthew Hart said it, and then Angharad knew the wisdom of her parents. The Welsh have lovely girl names, but they use them charily over here in America; it needs the Celtic soft and agile tongue to get around them, so they are left in the old family Bibles, names like Gwenllian, Myfanwy, Dilys, Morfydd, and, most of all, Angharad. There is such a protection for a girl in such a name, however, that Dai and Marged Evans called their first-born daughter so. They did know, coming out of Wales themselves, that it was worth all the Helens and the Loises, the Darlenes and the Lindas, for as much as if ever Angharad did ever meet the right man she would hear her name sing out from him. That is an old virtue of the Welsh girl names, that is worth all their lovely outlandishness.

Angharad was rising twenty-five, and she had never heard her name sing yet. As a ward nurse in University Hospital she had almost forgotten all about her name, and was content

enough with her boy friend's name for her; he called her
Beautiful, as indeed she was. On one Saturday afternoon, just
before she was due to go off duty her name rang out for her;
and her old beau, who was waiting at the gate, never saw her
more. She never even gave him a thought, ever again.

They brought Mattie Hart in from the ball park, all muddied
and bloodied and out like a doused candle. The last thing that
Mattie had remembered was going down to block Bonnello,
the Iowa forward, and the block had cleanly sent him into the
world of concentric circles and shining lights and ringing noises.
Just as they laid him on the bed and Angharad was bending
over him he began to come out of it like a diver up from the
fishy deep, and there framed in the fading circles and surrounded by the receding ringings Mattie saw Angharad.

"Hello, Angharad," Mattie said. The world went very still
for the girl at that. She did not know that for a year she had
been coming between Mattie and his books, that wherever she
went Mattie had been around too, watching her. He could tell
Angharad from a crowd by her way of walking and her way
of talking and her eyes of blue, by her fair, shining helmet of
hair, by her tidy ankles, and by her decent ways. Mattie
thanked God and Bonnello for sending him unconscious into
her ward, for he was the shy man where women were concerned, and he would never have had the gall to speak to her
if he had not been coming out of coma when he did so. "Hello,
Angharad." He said it again, and the Welsh girl felt it down
to the soles of her feet.

"Are you doing anything tonight, Angharad? Are you?" The
people who had carried Mattie in began to back out at this
stage. They didn't know what was going on, but they knew that
they were no part of it. Angharad sat down shakily on the edge
of the bed, against all her graduate training manuals, and just

beamed mistily at the coming-to Matthew. She knew, everybody on the campus knew, that Matthew Hart, the Scranton Irishman, was the thrust in the football attack. He was stocky and dark, with a serious face, and out of him was coming what she had always heard about — her name, Angharad. It was singing out of him. In a way Angharad became a woman from that moment.

She didn't answer Matthew. She didn't answer because she couldn't answer, but she nodded and shook her head in a way that Matthew understood, and it was only when she had promised to be in Shevlin Hall vestibule at 8 p.m. that either of them thought of wiping the blood and mud away from the still dazing Matthew.

There was nothing the matter with the lad, and he walked back to the Field House for a bath and a change before he realized that he had no boots on. He ate standing, jostled by his fellow ballplayers. Zatrick, a big moose of a second-string quarterback, with whom Mattie had been in the habit of moseying around on Saturday evenings, nuzzled up to him: "Are you coming out tonight, Matt? They're serving Bock beer down at Coughlan's, there's a new singer at the Flame Room. . . ." He went on talking until he saw that Matt was not even in the room with him, although his stocky body was still there.

Matthew was in the vestibule of Shevlin Hall about half an hour before he said that he would be there. Angharad knew right away when he did arrive, because she had planted one of her girl friends behind the potted palms to watch for him. She sailed down the stairs about three minutes late — that was as long as she could hang out, and she heard it again: "Hello, Angharad." Whenever she heard Angharad come from Mattie she knew what she was made for.

They went to the movies, and Mattie held her hand as if it was a live pigeon. They walked home, and for weeks and months every night when it was possible, they were together all their spare time.

Summer was coming in, and one evening, casually, seemingly, Angharad asked Matthew to come home with her for the week end. "To meet my people, you know, Mattie." He agreed equably enough, albeit rather grimly, because, although he and Angharad had bridged the gap, the Capulets and the Montagues were liable to be regarded as amicable relations compared to the Evanses and the Harts. There has always been a great difference between the Irish Catholic and the Welsh Nonconformist in every way. The sooner the two started to understand one another the better it would be, but Mattie felt, properly enough, that it was hard lines that the task had lit on him.

The Evanses had heard enough about Mattie in Angharad's consciously artless references to him in her letters to get the score. For a week before Angharad was due to bring him down from the university Mrs. Evans was polishing and baking, scolding and rehearsing with the family how to greet Angharad's young man. This was the first time that Angharad had brought a young man home with her, and Cathrin and Olwen, her younger sisters, still in high school, and Gwyn, her brother, on the railroad with his dad, were schooled in the way of the old ones as to how to greet a suitor who was coming to put his feet under the table for the first time. Mr. Evans tried to hide behind his newspaper, smoking his pipe, pretending that he was aloof from all the nonsense, but he used to lie awake at night, beside his sleeping wife, wondering, hoping for his lovely girl.

On Friday evening the Evanses were all in the living room

waiting for the roar past of the Greyhound bus. It stopped near
their door, and when it did they all got up and stood near the
door, twisting their hands, Cathy and Olwen nudging one
another, but warily watching for Mama's hand out of the slant
of their eyes.

The front door opened and in came Angharad and Matthew.
After kissing Mama and throwing her arms around Dada,
Angharad said, waving her arm up and down embarrassedly:
"Mama, Dada, Gwyn, kids, this is Matthew." Matthew almost
bowed as he shook hands with Mrs. Evans and Mr. Evans.
He shook hands with Gwyn, who tried to look at him under-
standingly, and only succeeded in looking at him conspirato-
rially, and he passed over the two girls lightly.

Then, to hide their awkwardness, everybody started to be
very hospitable. "Gwyn," said Mrs. Evans, bustling like mad,
"do you take Matthew's bag up to his room, and show him
where the upstairs bathroom is. Come along with me, Angharad. There is nice you do look, gel." And leading her fair
and eldest child into the bathroom off the living room she sat
on the side of the bath and lovingly watched while Angharad
washed and changed. As she sat there watching, she thought of
Matthew. No man would ever be good enough for her lovely
girl, that was for sure, but Matthew looked a steady decent
boy. She wished he didn't play that old football and was going
in for something genteel and prosperous, like medicine or
dentistry, but, she sighed, Rees the Grocer had put Dilwyn
in for medicine and Dil was always casting sheep's eyes at her
Angharad, but, she mentally shrugged, the flaccid Dilwyn was
no match for her Angharad. Sighing she got up from her un-
comfortable perch. While she had been cogitating her eyes had
never left Angharad, and one thing was certain to her, Angharad was in good shape, and Matthew was a decent lad. That

was all. Time would tell, but, Mrs. Evans hoped, time would tell before Angharad married her Matthew, for then it would be too late.

In the living room the table was all set for a real Welsh festal buffet supper. The table was groaning under a cooked ham, a whole cold turkey, a head cheese, and garnishes and side dishes, sauces and breads. Mr. Evans, to cover his shyness, was almost roaring hospitality at Matthew. "Sit here, Matthew, bachan, sit you here," pushing Matthew down beside a card table. Waving his carvers around, Mr. Evans said: "What will you have, lad, to start with? Some ham maybe, or some turkey?" He was waving his knife and fork, both huge and horn-handled, around like batons. All around Mattie the Evanses had disposed themselves, looking as longingly as they could decently do, especially Cathy and Olwen, at the lovely spread of food. Mattie licked his lips and said: "I'd like a piece of that cheese in the corner, by there, Mr. Evans, please." Mr. Evans looked around almost wildly, still waving his carvers, and there, in a corner of the table, cowering like a mouse under the ham, was a dried-up little piece of cheese, that Cathy, drat that Cathy! had put on the table by mistake.

Mr. Evans looked uncomprehendingly at Matthew. Matthew went on, "You see, Mr. Evans, I don't eat meat on Fridays." Angharad suddenly realized, with a start, that she had got so used to the fact that Mattie didn't eat meat on Fridays, that she had never even thought to mention it in writing home. Or maybe she did, but pretended she was forgetting. Whatever it was, here was the showdown.

The whole family was looking aghast at Matthew by this time, aghast at a man letting his vegetarian principles come between him and this bumper supper. Mrs. Evans said brightly, unknowingly, womanly: "There is a fine idea that you have,

Matthew, not to eat meat once a week. We all do eat too much meat, for sure, but why not not eat meat on Monday next, or Tuesday next, eh, lad?"

Matthew had caught his breath by this time. "No, Mrs. Evans," he said. "It must be Friday." And by dint of persuasion Matthew got all the others eating hard away at the meat while he swallowed down the dry piece of cheese with a cracker, pretending to enjoy it, almost the way that Charlie Chaplin had enjoyed the piece of leather in the *Gold Rush*. There was not much talking as the food was being champed, and the Evanses, barring Angharad, kept worrying within about Matthew and his cheese habit — moldy old cheese, when there was meat around.

Suddenly Gwyn looked up from his feeding. A thought had struck him. It excited him so much that in trying to express it he nearly went blue in the face, as the food kept struggling down his throat. He, forgetting his manners, pointed his fork straight at Matthew: "You're a Catholic, Mattie, that's what it is, isn't it? You're a Catholic!" That did it. There was a hush over all the room. Matthew carefully swallowed down the rest of his dry mouthful, looked at Gwyn quietly, grinned and said: "Yes, that's it. I'm Catholic. Mr. Evans, could you pass me some more of that cheese, please," and Matthew went on quietly, his eyes down, smiling a little, and waiting for events to take their course. He didn't look at Angharad, and she didn't look at him.

Mr. Evans cleared his throat. "Well, I knew a Catholic once. He was a nice fellow. You remember him, Mama, he used to take over from me at Milwaukee, Felix Weingarten?" Mrs. Evans, after one quick glance at Angharad, answered quickly, nervously. "Why, of course, I remember Mr. Weingarten." She went on, with great conviction: "He was a nice man."

Everything had come to a stop, with this knowledge of Matthew's faith. It all added up, though. He looked like a Catholic, all the Evanses thought, looking at Mattie and not meaning to. He was a Catholic Irish, that was for sure.

Mattie, quite composedly, to ease the awkward, not unfriendly silence, got up and said: "Excuse me a moment. I'm going upstairs for a moment," and away he went, up to the bathroom. The others went on eating. They were in a jumble. That was all they knew. Angharad just chewed away at the meat, silent, dogged, waiting for something to happen. Then it did.

There was a hell of a crash, as a heavy body came tumbling down the stairs. Mrs. Evans had been polishing only too well. As Matthew came out of the bathroom, having flushed the toilet needlessly for effect, slipped on the gleaming top step of the staircase, and came crashing down, turning two lumbering somersaults as he did so. He landed on his back in the hallway, and for a moment he was in a ringing darkness in a descending loom.

The family, after a moment's horrified pause, rushed to the bottom of the stairs and gathered around their tumbled guest, their Angharad's young man. As they were looking down on him Matthew opened his eyes, and slowly smiled, looking up at Angharad.

"Hello, Angharad," he said. And when he said that, all the worry and fretting went out of Dai and Marged Evans. For when Matthew said "Angharad" they knew their lovely girl was safe, safer than at her maiden home. It is an old virtue of the Welsh girl names, that only true love can give them all their loveliness, and the two of them heard what all the parents of girls pray to hear, their girl's name ringing.

# VI

## COO-CULLEN

A BOY there was in old Ireland, whose mother called him Salty. Nobody ever calls him Salty now, because the Irish people gave him another name, and it was under the new name that the boy became Ireland's pride, and England's envy, and the delight of the whole wide world. Salty's new name was Coo-Cullen, and in getting that name the young lad came to glory and to an early green grave in Ireland.

It happened a long time ago, before America, when Ireland was the Western World. To look at him nobody would ever have given Salty a second glance. He was a small dark lad. He had a gentle way with him, and his eyes were sad and blue. Although he was only a little fellow, his mother loved him dearly; for he was all she had after the boy's father was killed in some local trouble. There was always some trouble in Ireland in those days. They lived in Ulster, which is the north of Ireland, and the men of Ulster were always fighting against the men of the west of Ireland, or against the men of the south of Ireland, or against the men of Scotland, who were some sort of cousins of theirs. There was always a fight going on somewhere, and while it's fun to read about fighting, and while the men were always itching after it, it's a sad and bitter thing for the mothers and the children. So Salty's mother brought him up in a quiet place, and like all mothers she prayed that her little boy would never have to go to the wars. Besides, Salty was such a little fellow.

As Salty grew into boyhood he began to see that his mother was keeping something from him. He loved his mother, but he was restless in that quiet place, and at last he went to her.

"Mother, why are there no other boys here for me to play with?"

His mother looked at him sadly for a while and then she said:

"They are living at the King's House, Salty."

Salty looked at her straight, and because he knew it would pain her he said no more, but the next morning he went to her with his stick and his ball and told her that he was going to the King's House, to see what the boys were doing. His mother nodded slowly and did not try to stop him. She just pointed to the west, where the King's House lay, then turned away so that Salty would not see her weeping.

Salty faced the west, threw the ball in the air, and hit it with his stick. As it soared westward through the clear air he ran after it, and so fleet was he that he always caught it before it reached the ground. All day long he traveled that way, and as the quiet of Christ was coming over Ulster with the gentle fall of evening he came to the fields that surrounded the King's House.

There were a crowd of boys playing in the fields. The game they were playing was a sort of hockey, and Salty watched them for a minute and then ran in to join them. Before any of them could stop him he guided the ball with his stick and scored a goal. When the boys saw that he was a stranger they crowded around him, and Salty could feel in the air their dislike of him. They were all big redheaded boys, whose fathers had become the bosses in Ulster, while Salty, small and dark, was evidently just a poor native boy.

The leader of the redheads looked Salty over silently. None of the others said anything; they just kept shuffling around Salty, who was scared inside, but didn't show it. He just stared back at the crowding gang.

"Who are you?" said the gang leader at last, slowly, and with menace.

"My name is Salty," he said. "I've never had friends to play with, so I came to join you. But I can see that you don't want me, so I'll be on my way." Salty tried to push his way through the crowd of them, carrying his stick and his ball with him, because he didn't want any trouble. All his life he never was to go looking for trouble. It always was to make him feel sick and trembly when it started.

"Just a minute, Darky, just a minute," said the gang leader easily. "Did you think you were going to get away with it like that? We're going to teach you little local boy not to come around bothering us." Then, before Salty could put his hands up, all the gang started to hit him on his shoulders and his arms with their sticks.

Salty ran a little way to get clear of them, and this, of course, made the gang bolder. It always makes a gang bolder when they see that their victim is a weak one, so they ran after him, howling and jostling one another to get a crack at the gossoon. They would have killed him in their excitement, and that would have been all right, because Salty was just a native of the place. The poor deluded redheads began to enjoy themselves, when, all of a sudden, Salty turned and faced them. Even then, in his first fight, all new to the game, Salty somehow knew where to fight. He stopped to face them on a wee hillock, that gave him an advantage in height, and behind him was a rock, so that they couldn't sneak around the back of him.

If the gang hadn't been so excited and confident they would have seen something in Salty that would have made them want to talk things over. The small diffident shy boy had suddenly become a squat, crouched, and hunched little fighter, who held his stick as if it was part of him. Salty's nostrils had flared out, and his pallor had become dead white. Something seemed to come out of him, a sort of power, as it still does, out of all great fighters.

As the first redhead reached him, Salty gave a wordless scream and he hit his tormentor so hard that the boy went down. A joy entered into Salty, and he struck and thrust at his enemies until they all realized that they were in the hands of a master fighting man. They broke and ran, those that were left standing, and with a whoop of sheer joy Salty ran after them. For sanctuary they sought the King's House, and they dashed past the astounded King Connor, upsetting the game of chess that he was enjoying with one of his advisers. Before the King had time to say anything Salty was in the hall after them. He chased his loutish tormentors all around the hall, while they wept and howled for mercy. Only when his anger was satisfied did Salty notice the King, who was staring at him open mouthed.

Salty leaned upon his stick and bowed like an actor, as his mother had taught him.

"It is King Connor, isn't it?" he asked politely, above the sobbing and the howling and the groaning. Salty always had a dignified way with him "Who are you? What's your name? Where are you from? What have you done?" The questions poured out of the King.

"My name is Salty. My father was a soldier, now dead. I come from Enniskillen to join the boys at your house, but they beat me up until I got angry. I'm sorry if I have disturbed you. I'll be on my way now," said Salty. "I had hoped to stay."

The King had no intention of letting Salty go. He was a great warrior himself, and he saw the greatness that lay in Salty. "Let you be staying, dark lad. You have to be recommended to live in my house, but I'll recommend you myself. You'll stay here as Protector of the King's Boys, and one day you will lead them as my Household Brigade."

Salty smiled at the King, and the King smiled back. The gang had all crept away during this, and Salty bowed again to King Connor and went to the Boys' House, where he sat at the head of the table as by right. Within a few days all the redheads were his followers, and Salty was on his way to gaining his name of Coo-Cullen.

A local man named Cullen invited King Connor and a few of his friends to dinner one night. Cullen lived in a castle about ten miles from the King's House, and when the King was ready to start he shouted for Salty to come with him. Salty was in the middle of a game at the time, so he told the King to start without him, and that he would get there later. So the King and his friends drove off in their chariots, and Salty, about half an hour later, ran after them on foot. It was dark before he got to Cullen's castle, and he was still about a mile away when the assembled company was having a drink before their meal. The King didn't mention that Salty was coming, he didn't think of it; so Cullen locked the door of the castle and set his watchdog loose.

This animal was one of the wonders of Ireland. It wasn't a dog at all, but a black panther that some sailors had brought to Cullen out of Africa while it was still a helpless baby.

Cullen had trained it to prowl around the castle at night and to go back to its cage in the morning. It kept the wolves away from the flocks and the cattle, and only killed them itself when it was hungry, which Cullen thought was fair enough. The one great snag about the thing was that once the creature was loose it was impossible to get in or out of the castle until it went back to its lair, and was locked in, in the morning. The Irish word for hound was *Coo,* and that was what the panther was called — Coo-Cullen, or Cullen's hound.

Suddenly, while the company was drinking, a bloodcurdling snarl went up from the panther, and King Connor went pale at the sound of it, for he suddenly remembered Salty, and he on his way to the castle. The whole company grew silent at the snarling, which suddenly bayed into the shrieks that a panther makes before the kill. Salty was almost on top of the long and sinewy beast before he realized his danger. Almost without thinking he threw the pebble that he had been balancing in his hand so that it whizzed past the panther. The animal deflected its gaze a moment to look at it, and at that very moment Salty leaped to the side of the panther, and grabbing it by the scruff of the neck and by a hind leg he swung it up and around and dashed it against the castle wall. The panther snarled and spat and writhed like a mad thing, but Salty was inexorable. He killed the panther by repeated dashings, the whole two hundred pounds of panther, and when Cullen and King Connor, with torchbearers and many spears, dashed out to recover the lacerated body of Salty before the panther could drag it away, they found the small dark lad looking down at the broken, still twitching body of Cullen's hound.

It was from that time that Salty began to be regarded as different from all other men, as indeed he was. The King looked at him strangely for a while, and pityingly. Then he put his arm around Salty and led him into the castle.

Cullen, a decent stupid man, was inconsolable about the death of his panther. He knew that his flocks and herds would now be ravaged by the wolves, and that all the robbers of the area would endanger him now that his protection was gone, for trusting in his panther Cullen had no guards to protect him. He looked so glum, although relieved at Salty's safety, that Salty, touched with pity for him, said, "Cullen, send to Africa for another such a creature. Until he gets here and is trained, I, Salty, will be your watchdog."

So it was. For over a year, until the new panther was ready, Salty prowled the castle grounds every night. He kept away the beasts of prey and the robbers, who, after their first attempt against him, would have sooner gone against an army with banners than against that small, dark sad man. That was how Salty got the name of Coo-Cullen. He was the hound of Cullen. He was that man's protection as he was later to be the champion of all the people of Ireland, before his brief life was spent.

# VII

## COO-CULLEN GROWING UP

IT WAS a year and more before Cullen got hold of a new panther, and all that time Salty was his watchdog. He was never to be a big man, but the time he was at Cullen's made him strong and bold and hardy. After the wolves had come down on the flocks several times, Salty got so that he could run after them and catch them. All the little children and the peaceful people slept quietly in their beds every night because they knew that Coo-Cullen would keep harm from them; and bad men paled when they even heard his name. Cullen was sorry to see him go, and wanted him to stay and live with him, but the small dark boy had to press on toward his end.

When he went back to King Connor he took on where he had left off, but he found no joy in it. The boys of the King's House at once hailed him as their leader again, but Coo-Cullen felt that he was just marking time there. He knew that he was on the eve of great events that would change him, and so it happened.

King Connor used to ask any famous men who were passing through his country to come and talk to the boys, so that they would not grow up ignorant. And one day in the spring a famous wise man from the ancient land of Wales arrived to tell them about the future. The Welshman was very old, with a long white beard, and he had seen so much of the past that it was easy for him to tell what was going to happen ahead. He had a high singsong voice. When he was talking he didn't seem to be looking at anything, but his burning bright eyes, under their bushy white brows, seemed to be staring inward at what really mattered, under the surface of things.

"This day," said he, "a hero will arise in some land. Today he will take up arms for the first time, and he will start on his road to glory. His life will be a brief and bitter one, but the generations who come after him will always remember him." With that he looked straight at Coo-Cullen, for Salty was always called that now; and without a word Salty got up and went to King Connor.

Without even a salutation the dark lad said: "King, I no longer am a boy, but today I must take up arms as a man." King Connor looked at him sadly, for he loved the boy more than he did his own flesh and blood.

"Must you so, Coo-Cullen? Must you so? Ah well, neither myself or any other man can stop you. Is it the wise man from Wales who has been talking to you, and telling you this?"

Unsmiling Coo-Cullen said: "It is so." With a sigh the King shouted for his armor sergeant to come and equip the swank young lad with all the trappings of a warrior.

The soldiers of Erin were not like the knights in armor who came along later. They used to wear a kilt of saffron color, a cloak, and shoes like moccasins. Their weapons were a big broad sword that was called a claymore, a throwing spear, and a slingshot. To protect themselves they carried a round shield covered with thick cowhide and studded with nails. They didn't ride on horses, but used to drive a span of them harnessed to a chariot, that was an open low-slung light cart, and long knives used to project out from it, to cut enemies down if they tried to stop them driving through.

The armor sergeant brought out some good weapons for Coo-Cullen to try. Very seriously and earnestly Coo-Cullen tried them all, and none of them were good enough for him. He had to have the best, he knew. He simply could not afford to take chances on faulty weapons any more than a soldier or a farmer today can take chances with the tools of his trade. Coo-Cullen was so strong that the swords and the spears broke in his hands, as he tried them out quietly but furiously. The span of horses in the chariot could not keep up the furious pace that he set, and the cart itself came to pieces as he stamped up and down. The armor sergeant was in despair, until King Connor ordered out his own personal equipment. He knew that he would never be needing it anyhow as long as Coo-Cullen lived. The King's weapons and his horses and his chariot were the best that had ever been made up to that time, and they stood up to Coo-Cullen's testing. At last he was satisfied with his arms and equipment. Standing up in the chariot the boy pulled the horses up so that they reared, and, saluting the King, Coo-Cullen drove off to the borders of Ulster to look for glory. He went so fast that it looked as if a cloud of dust was traveling, and not a small dark sad lad driving furiously to look for immortality. Old-timers standing about swore that they could see a kind of glowing radiance all around the charioteer as he raced southward, out of Ulster. Be that as it may it is told as a fact that the speed of his passing raised a wind that tore washing off the lines and loosened shingles in the roofs.

Coo-Cullen didn't stop until he got to the border, where he pulled up the lathering horses to talk to one of the champions of Ulster. In those days, all along the border, where there was a pass between the mountains of Mourne, King Connor had placed his special men. If a man wanted to enter Ulster

as a friend, why that was fine and dandy, but if he came
looking for trouble, why, the champions would take him on
with no holds barred. Yet these champions were never bully
boys. They were always gentle with the weak and the poor and
with women and children, and if a traveling Irishman didn't
feel in the mood for fighting they were glad to send him on
his way in peace, or to sit and drink with him until he felt
natural again.

This particular champion was very fond of Coo-Cullen
and he warned him not to go out of Ulster that night, as
three bad men were hiding in the hills nearby, and they were
very hard hombres indeed, but at that Coo-Cullen's eyes lighted
up so that they seemed to be sparking, and without a word
he set his horses galloping toward the hills that were already
becoming blue in the evening light.

Coo-Cullen had never fought with real men before. Until
now he had been an apprentice. Now he wanted to see how
well he had learned his trade. His chariot swooped up the
mountain toward the glow of a campfire, outside a cave, which
he knew must be the hide-out of the bandits. As he drew up
with a swirl that almost set the horses back on their buttocks,
one of the bandits came out of the cave and stood looking
at him. Behind him his two brothers crowded. They laughed
when they saw the small dark man step down from his chariot
and start walking toward them, his hands hanging loose, his
sword by his side, and his spear and his shield on his back.
Coo-Cullen walked very lightly, like a cat, like all fighting
creatures, and he was obviously looking for trouble, and the
bandits thought that they were the boys who could give it to
him.

In those days, before men tangled with one another, they
always told the world who they were if there was time, and

by the light of the fire that evening it seemed as if there were plenty of time.

Coo-Cullen stopped a few paces from the fire, on the other side from the bandits, and thumping his chest with a thud he said: "I am Coo-Cullen, a champion man out of Ulster." Then he stayed quiet, very quiet, watching and waiting, in the flickering firelight. Night had come on by this time, and outside the circle of firelight all was dark and still. The hills around were watchful, everlasting, and waiting. The birds had lifted their heads from beneath their wings and were waiting too, but never broke the silence. The deer looked up from their couches in the heather, and the solitary wildcat, crouched on a jutting rock, gazed unblinking at the small dark man making his brag.

The first bandit stepped forward and he thumped his chest. "I am Brian Boy McGee and my father was Owen Downy, and I care nothing for all the men of Ulster. My father, God rest him, used to eat three Ulstermen before his breakfast on a quiet morning."

With that he struck at Coo-Cullen with a razor-sharp sword that he had craftily concealed behind his back, but with a gasp saw that Coo-Cullen was no longer there. The lithe dark hero had leaped aside as the blade descended, and the blanket of the dark had covered him. Brian Boy looked around wildly for his enemy when with an awful whistle a slingshot came whizzing in from the black night, and it stretched him senseless on the ground.

The second brother stepped over the still body of the first and made his brag, and his voice sounded raucous in the still night air. "I am Red Marty McGee," said he, "and my brother is Brian Boy. He was betrayed by the wiles of a crafty black Ulsterman."

Coo-Cullen was not to be seen. He had become a part of the dark night. Then suddenly a splash of water landed on the fire, and in the smoke and sparks that came up, while Red Marty was spluttering, Coo-Cullen leaped at him and beat him thrice over the head with the flat of his sword, and the second bandit joined his brother in sleeping.

The third and last of the bandits stepped forward warily over the quiet bodies of his two brothers and he beat his chest and bragged: "I am Rory of the Battles, and no small dark man can beat me." But the poor fellow said it without spirit, and he even bowed his head so that Coo-Cullen could reach up to smite him, for he was a fine tall redheaded man, and until that night he had had a great opinion of himself. Then when the three of them lay empty of harm Coo-Cullen tended his horses and gave them grass and water. The creatures of the wild ceased their watching, and the night took over while Coo-Cullen stamped out the fire, woke up the three sore-headed bandits, and tied them behind his chariot. As he drove back through the gloom of middle night he remembered his deeds, and his heart was high with them, and a great feeling of peace came over Coo-Cullen.

He drove slowly through the darkness, and as dawn was breaking he came again to the country around the household of King Connor. In the early light he saw a noble stag, that was as big as a moose. He couldn't chase it in his chariot, as the bandits were tethered behind, and anyhow the horses were not fast enough to keep up with the fleet-footed stag, so he leaped out and chased it on foot. So fast was Coo-Cullen that he ran past the stag, and turned and tackled it. He jumped upon its back when it got up, and although it bucked and reared like a steer he mastered it, and rode it quietly back to his chariot and harnessed it to the front to help the tired horses.

Just as he did so a flight of black swans passed overhead. Now these were very unusual birds, so Coo-Cullen made a mighty leap into the blue air and caught three of them in his hands. He tied them so that they flew above his chariot, and so he came home to King Connor.

Coo-Cullen in his day had done wonders. Although he was to do far more glorious things in the brief span of life that was left to him, King Connor was always to remember that shining spring morning when the dark, unsmiling lad with the quiet hands hove into sight, all gilded by the rising sun, in his chariot, with the black swans circling over him, the stag stepping out with the horses, and the three bandits plodding along in the rear.

All Ulster knew, then all of Ireland knew, that a hero had arisen in the North. The small, dark sad man, who had been the guardian of Cullen's castle, was to become the guardian of all of Ulster, then of all of Ireland, and, in a way, of all the Western World.

# VIII

## THE CATTLE RAID ON COOLEY

IN THE days when Coo-Cullen was in his pride there was no money at all. If any Irishman in those days had seen a dollar bill he would never have known it. The rich men in those days were the men who had the best cattle or the fastest horses or a singing voice or the wisdom to tell about the future. The voice might crack, and the wisdom might fail, and the horses might stumble, so that the wealth that was most desired was cattle, and it was the greedy search for wealth by Maeve the Queen of Ireland that brought Coo-Cullen to his doom.

Ever since he had proved himself, Coo-Cullen had been the champion of King Connor, and he had regarded the King as his own father; while King Connor on his part loved Coo-Cullen more than his own sons. King Connor owned the best bull in Ireland. It was a huge, brown beast of a bull, and it was his pride and joy. So famous was it that Queen Maeve was greedy to get it, and once a bad and wealthy person sets their heart on something there is always trouble until it is obtained. There is no joy in such getting, just dirty greed.

Queen Maeve first tried to buy the brown bull legally, but King Connor would not even talk terms. He sent her messengers away rubbing their ears; he had clipped them across the head for their impudence in even asking for the bull. So Queen Maeve turned to trickery in order to get the bull. She didn't want the big, brown brute because she was a cattle fancier; she was just determined that nobody else should have any better stock than she possessed.

In order to do her dirty work she sent across to Wales, where some very crafty people lay hiding from the anger of King Connor, who had booted them out of Ulster, because, he said, they were not fit to associate with decent men. One of the villains was a man named Mickey Finn, and he proposed a scheme to Queen Maeve that met with her approval. The scheme was this: to send some drugged liquor to King Connor, all wrapped up in a fancy packet, the liquor to be drugged so strongly that it would put the King and all his warriors to sleep for a whole year, and in their sleeping Queen Maeve could cross the border into Ulster, rustle the bull, and put all Ulster to destruction at the same time.

It was just the sort of dirty trick that appealed to Queen Maeve, and the parcel, all fancy, was prepared and sent to King Connor right away. The label was forged, so that it looked as if it had come from the King of Scotland, who brewed the best liquor in the world in those days; he still does for that matter. Now King Connor, like most Irishmen, God help them, could never say no to a drink, and he and his men had a fine party on the stuff the night the parcel of liquor arrived. All his men passed into the deep sleep with him, except Coo-Cullen, who never touched the stuff. He was away hunting at the time anyway.

Mickey Finn had sneaked into Ulster disguised as a decent man, and as soon as he saw that King Connor and his men had fallen for his trick he sent a swift messenger off to Queen Maeve, who was standing near the borders of Ulster, ready to march in with her army.

Coo-Cullen returned a few hours after the King and his

company had fallen into their slumber. He knew at once that something was the matter when he saw the whole of the host of Ulster all stretched out in the dining hall, fast asleep and fully dressed. Without wasting a moment he jumped into his chariot and rushed to the border just as the sly Queen Maeve was preparing to cross the river that led into Ulster. It was night when Coo-Cullen reached the other side of the river. He left his chariot with his driver, and swam across to where the whole army of Ireland was sleeping, with its sentries thrown out to guard them.

The first thing that Coo-Cullen did was to corral all the sentries and hang them up from a tree, like a line of washing. The poor fellows were so terrified when they realized that they were being handled by the great Coo-Cullen, the Hound of Ulster, that they hung quiet all night, with their eyes bugging out, afraid to whisper even to each other as they swung upside down in the gentle night breeze. Then Coo-Cullen cut down a mighty tree with his sword. He peeled the bark off it so that it looked like a telegraph pole, and he sharpened one end of it, which he stuck into the middle of the swirling river, and on it he pinned a notice saying "Keep Out, Tricky Maeve," and he signed it Coo-Cullen, the Hound of Ulster. That was the first time that Coo-Cullen had ever signed himself the Hound of Ulster, but he knew that night that the whole safety of the women and children of Ulster was his responsibility, so he felt again the way he had felt when he was Cullen's watchdog, only he felt it a thousand times more on this dangerous occasion.

In those days the way through Ireland was all tangled and wooded, so in the morning Queen Maeve sent a party of her engineers to survey the river and to come back and report to her. The wicked woman was in great spirits, because she felt that in no time at all the famous brown bull of Cooley would join her herd, to the sorrow of King Connor.

The morning dawned fine and early, and the engineers soon reached the riverbank after the first light had broken. No sooner had they seen the warning notice on the pole than Coo-Cullen was raging among them, and he had knocked all of them cold before they even had had a chance to know whether it was a thunderbolt or the small dark hero that had struck them. Coo-Cullen could not take any prisoners, as he had no place to put them, nor any men to guard them, with all the Ulster warriors doped by Mickey Finn, so he tied them into a cart and smacked the horses on the rump, having pointed them in the general direction of Queen Maeve's camp.

The slippery woman was standing in the doorway of her tent, eagerly waiting for the return of her engineers, when the driver-less wagon clattered past her door with the dazed engineers just beginning to sit up and take notice in the body of it. She let out a screech when she saw them that stopped the horses and brought all the camp running to the place. "What's the matter with youse all?" she screamed; she was a very uneducated woman, that same Maeve. "What's the matter with youse all? Are youse all drunk, you dirty engineers?" But the poor men could only chatter and jibber like monkeys, for they had begun to realize that they had been in the hands of the great Coo-Cullen, and had got away with it. At last they could tell the story, how they had seen a huge pole stuck in the river, with a notice on it, but before they had been even able to start reading it something had hit them. The whole camp murmured and shuffled, for none of them had the heart to move against Ulster if Coo-Cullen had escaped the wiles of Mickey Finn.

Queen Maeve's eyes glittered with hate against the small dark man who alone stood between her and the brown bull of

Cooley. Her hands writhed like a nest of snakes, and she bit her lips until the blood ran, trying to think of a way of overcoming the single obstacle that lay between her and her greedy desire. She stormed and ranted at her men, and strung up poor Mickey Finn to the nearest tree. Then she sent a troop of cavalry to fight its way to the river, to read the notice and report back to her, but they never came back; they had met Coo-Cullen in his anger, the poor unfortunate fellows. At last the whole army moved ponderously to the river, cautiously and fearfully, and even then Coo-Cullen circled around them like the hound that he was and snapped up any stragglers, who never saw their mothers again.

At last Queen Maeve got to the riverbank and read the notice that was fluttering on the pole. When she read the words "Keep Out, Tricky Maeve," she fell into such an angry fit that she foamed at the mouth and swore that she would never rest until she saw Coo-Cullen dead.

Coo-Cullen watched her tantrums from the branches of a high tree, and he saw her go into conference with her generals. Some of those same generals were decent men, friends of Coo-Cullen in the days before Maeve by her beguiling, because she was a very beautiful, as well as a very bad woman, had subjugated all of Ireland to her will except for the land of Ulster. At the conference she demanded that some of the generals should visit Coo-Cullen and ask him what he wanted, under a flag of truce. She offered to give him all the wealth he wanted; she even promised to spare all of Ulster, just as long as he let her take away the brown bull.

The generals shook their heads. "Queen Maeve," they said, "you will never be able to bribe or to beguile the dark lad. That Coo-Cullen is the cleanest man who ever lived, and he will have to die before he lets you pass into Ulster. There are not enough cattle in the world, nor enough horses, to buy the small dark man. He will defend his land of Ulster against hell and high water, against the rest of Ireland, until the dope wears off King Connor and his fighting men." Queen Maeve sneered at them.

"Every man can be bought," she said. "Didn't I buy all of youse bold heroes?" The poor generals shuffled and looked ashamed. "Let you go, Darky, and you, Skin-Horn. You both used to be friends of Coo-Cullen. Tell him that I'll give him anything he wants. I'll even marry him to my daughter, and I'll resign, so that he can be king of Ireland, just so long as I get that brown bull out of Ulster. BUT I'M GOING TO GET THAT BULL!"

Darky and Skin-Horn crossed the river under a flag of truce, and they found Coo-Cullen waiting for them, standing by his chariot. They got a lump in their throat, as they looked at the small dark man standing beside his horses and his driver, so composed and quiet as always. He greeted them with quiet affection, for he knew that soldiers often have to serve under leaders that they never like.

"Coo-Cullen," said Darky, after the salutations were over, "Coo-Cullen, Queen Maeve wants to know what your terms are." Darky never looked at Coo-Cullen while he spoke those words.

"These are my terms," said Coo-Cullen. "Queen Maeve must supply me with food, as I will have no time to prepare it, and I will let her army advance for as far and as long every day as it takes me to beat one of her champions every day. If I am disabled, why, as you know, all Ulster will be at her mercy. If she doesn't agree I'll harass and kill her army from the bushes while I have life in me, and I'll slaughter the bull of Cooley, so that there will be no point in her going on at all unless she agrees to my terms. I have given this matter great thought," said Coo-Cullen seriously, "and it seems to me the only way that I can hold the wicked Maeve at bay until King Connor and his army awake."

"But Coo! my dear friend," said Skin-Horn impulsively. "Sure, you can't do that! It will be at least a full six months before Mickey Finn's dirty work wears away, and how can you fight all the champions of Ireland, one a day for six months? Why don't you give her the bull, and become king of Ireland?" Coo-Cullen shook his small, dark, sad head.

"No, my dear companions, that cannot be. Let you go back with my message, and I pray that we will never meet in battle, for it would be a drear thing to fall by the hand of one of you."

The generals went back to camp with Coo-Cullen's message. Queen Maeve grinned all over her face when she heard it. Early next morning the army prepared to move across the river while one of her chief bully boys went out to engage Coo-Cullen. Coo-Cullen was still such a young hero that many of the more famous old-time champions were scornful of meeting him, and his friends, of course, didn't want to tangle with the small dark man; they still loved life. On the first morning, then, while the Irish army looked on, a bold, young fighting man out of Cork, where many great fighters have always come from, was rowed across the river to meet Coo-Cullen. He stood up before the dark lad, all armed and confident, and began to make his brag, when Coo-Cullen stopped him. "Wait now, Corkman, wait now," said Coo-Cullen courteously. "Have you thought this over, lad? We are fighting for keeps, you know. Let you be going away from here now, or you'll go back over the river feet first." This quiet, conciliatory speech of Coo-Cullen so angered the Cork lad that he made a terrific swipe at Coo-Cullen with his sword. The small, sad Ulsterman side-stepped it cautiously, and bringing his own sword down like a scythe he cut the earth from underneath the feet of the fighting man from Cork. He didn't want to harm the young lad. The roars of the crowd so angered the Corkman, however, that he would not stop, but rushed on Coo-Cullen with a wild fighting scream. Coo-Cullen tried to stop him again by flashing his sword across his head so closely that he cut off the Corkman's hair, but still the Corkman wouldn't stop, so, with a sigh, Coo-Cullen cut him down.

The army did not get far that day, nor the next day, nor the next. Coo-Cullen sadly killed all the champions that Maeve sent against him, so that in five months the Irish army had barely got more than five miles the other side of the river, and over a hundred of the best fighting men had been killed. Queen Maeve was livid with fury. She began to send Coo-Cullen's old friends against him, and in the middle of the fifth month she demanded that Darky go against Coo-Cullen. It was a dour and bloody fight that resulted. Darky had to be killed by Coo-Cullen, and it was agony to the small dark hero to do it, but in dying Darky badly wounded Coo-Cullen.

Coo-Cullen had been fighting now every day, except Sundays, for over five months, and the small, dark man was wearing down. He had been wounded several times, and he never had had a chance to get the wounds attended to. It was looking black for Coo-Cullen as well as for the women and children of Ulster, not forgetting the brown bull of Cooley, and then Maeve pulled her trump card. She sent for Skin-Horn, and sent him out against Coo-Cullen.

The nearest approach to Coo-Cullen in the world was this same Skin-Horn. He was Coo-Cullen's dearest friend. They had been raised together in the court of King Connor, but Queen

Maeve injected a poison into Skin-Horn's veins so that he thought that Coo-Cullen had murdered Darky, who was their mutual friend, and Skin-Horn, all furious and misled, went out, fresh and angry and souped-up, to fight against Coo-Cullen who was tired and sad at the slaughter that he had had to perform, and was more weary than any mortal man has a right to be.

That fight was one of the bitterest the world has ever seen. It went on for three whole days, during which the Irish army crept further and further into Ulster. It was so furious a fight that the shields gave way at the seams, and both Coo-Cullen and Skin-Horn broke their swords. So close had Coo-Cullen and Skin-Horn been as friends that they knew one another's plays, and Coo-Cullen was wounded near to death, poor, tired small man, before, with a sob, he finally dealt the mortal blow to Skin-Horn. The Irish army stopped again, and Maeve ordered another champion to meet Coo-Cullen in the morning, and to finish him off. Coo-Cullen was near to death that night.

In the morning, try as he would, he could not rise from his couch of heather. The only ones of King Connor's court, besides Coo-Cullen, that had escaped the trick of Mickey Finn were the brigade of boys who were training there, and in the morning they boldly placed themselves between the rest of Ulster and the prevailing Irish. Now the Irish would not normally fight against boys, but they had been trying to get into Ulster for five long months now, so they took the boys on, while the bleeding Coo-Cullen, with a broken leg and a fractured arm, dealt him by Skin-Horn, watched in helpless agony while all the boys went down to death for Ulster. Still, their heroism saved the day, for they held off the Irish army for a whole long and bloody week, and the glory of their dying raised such a keen of sorrow among the mothers of Ulster that it awakened King Connor and the warriors from their doped sleep, and just in time the Ulstermen arrived at the scene of the battle of the Boys' Brigade to avenge them, and to drive Queen Maeve and her army headlong out of Ulster.

Coo-Cullen recovered from his many wounds and became the darling of Ulster, but his natural sadness was made even more pronounced by the death of his young Boys' Brigade and by the killing of his friends by his hand. Slowly, and too late, Coo-Cullen realized that the glory of being a great warrior was a bitter sort of sweetness. Too late he realized that although he was destined for glory, and had won great renown, the price of such fame was out of all proportion. It was too late to turn back at that time, even had he wanted to. Queen Maeve had sworn revenge, and had offered her kingdom to any man who could overcome Coo-Cullen. It was the hate of this evil woman that was to bring the Hound of Ulster to his death, for no swordsman can fight against the wiles of a foul queen as Coo-Cullen was to find out, to his sorrow and to his everlasting glory.

Queen Maeve's cattle raid on Cooley failed because of Coo-Cullen and the heroism of the boys of Ulster, but had King Connor known what was to result he would have given Queen Maeve the brown bull, and would have served her as a slave himself. But men never can tell what lies ahead, and that is both a sorrow and a blessing to mankind, as will be seen from the next story.

# IX

## THE END OF COO-CULLEN

ALL good things come to an end, and they generally end far too soon, while bad things tend to linger on. So it was with Coo-Cullen, to the sorrow of his people. He came to his death when most young men are thinking of starting to live, but instead of thinking about a girl with shining hair and a houseful of children poor Coo-Cullen had to fight the lonely and bitter fight against the Death-Man that all men must undergo sooner or later, but always better later. He had no family around him when he died, but only an unfriendly and hating enemy, and his only creature companions were the lonely badger and the greedy vulture.

It was Queen Maeve who brought Coo-Cullen to his death. She had never forgiven him since the time that he had stopped her from raging through Ulster with her army, and from rustling the brown bull of Cooley. She swore she would get him, and because hate makes people mad she was content to rot forever as long as she could put out the shining light of honor that was the small dark Ulster hero. All over the world she sent her servants to gather schemes to fix Coo-Cullen. Her servants were very wary about accepting any scheme unless it was tried and true, for they all had the unfortunate Mickey Finn still hanging in their mind's eye. At last all the schemes were gathered together and pondered upon, and then they were used against Coo-Cullen.

First Queen Maeve started a whispering campaign against the lad. Because he was shy and never boastful the rumor went around that Coo-Cullen was getting high and mighty, and too proud to talk to the common people of Ulster. The whispers reached Coo-Cullen, and they hurt him more than any wound had ever done, but he could no more talk about the sadness that such rumors caused him than he could boast about his feats of arms. A bad person always has an advantage over a good person for that very reason, because no ordinary decent man will ever argue hotly against lies that are told about him; he will just let them fester in his heart, and that is why lying and talebearing is far more sinful than the honest clout or the shouted curse.

When the whispering campaign was going really well, Queen Maeve imported some horrid experts in the arts of lying. These liars came from Wales, and they moved around the people and told them that Coo-Cullen had killed all his best friends, as indeed he had, but they said that he had killed them by tricks and poison because he was jealous and afraid of them. The people began to believe the liars. If any liar is impudent enough, and the lie is told often enough, people tend to believe it, especially if it is a preposterous one. Gradually the people began to avoid Coo-Cullen's company, and the small dark man was deeply hurt by the defection of his own people. More and more he tended to keep himself to himself, and he and his driver used to spend weeks, alone, out hunting in the woods. The more he avoided people the more the people believed the lies that were told about him. The one man who would never listen to any words against Coo-Cullen was King

Connor himself, and he suffered more than Coo-Cullen, for in many ways he was the more sensitive man of the two. Moreover King Connor, although a great and a famous warrior, had had a far happier and fuller life than poor Coo-Cullen, because he was born to it, whereas poor Coo-Cullen had had to choose one thing or the other. King Connor was worried about Coo-Cullen, but there is nothing that even a king can do for his friend if the people turn against him. People are the most important people, far more important than kings or heroes, once a lot of them get a fixed idea into their heads, like the French did when they threw the king down, or like the Americans, when they soaked the tea.

Queen Maeve wasn't just after Coo-Cullen, she was also after all of Ulster, and the great King Connor. She knew that words alone would never wear Coo-Cullen down, so she had her soldiers trained in all the ways of war, and she imported experts to teach them all the fighting tricks. She was quite happy about the way things were going, with the schools of swordplay and the spearing, until a wee, black fellow came in to call one day with a contraption that put all the rest of the fighting ways out of her mind for good and all. The wee, black man was a pygmy out of darkest Africa, and he showed Queen Maeve how a blowpipe and a poisoned dart could lay low the mightiest warrior, although the man behind the blowpipe was no bigger than the pygmy himself. Queen Maeve just refused to believe the little blackamoor until he coaxed her into letting him challenge any warrior of her court to combat. At first none of the swank heroes would even bother to accept the pygmy challenge, until at length Queen Maeve ordered black McCarthy to try out against the little stranger. No sooner did McCarthy start to rush against him, waving his sword, than the little pygmy put the blowpipe to his lips and — Puff! — the dart entered McCarthy's chest and he lay down stiff as a board for all eternity.

Queen Maeve gave the black man plenty of money for the blowpipe-poison-dart process, and she put the weapon into immediate production, and equipped all her army with it. It was a dirty thing to do, but it was what was to be expected of that wicked woman. After that it wasn't only poisoned words but poisoned darts that she was pointing against Coo-Cullen. It's a good thing to know that it is even among the Irish themselves there were such villains. The English could not be blamed for all these mean actions, because the English were still swinging from tree to tree at this time when the Irish were all so civilized as to be using propaganda and poison.

By the time her army was all equipped and ready to march against Ulster, which never regarded itself as a part of Ireland but as a place set apart, the only friend that Coo-Cullen had in the world was King Connor. Of course his mother still loved him, but mothers will always love their sons in any case, and his driver also loved Coo-Cullen, but that was different. The driver loved Coo-Cullen because he was such a famous man to serve, so that the only real friend was the King, Connor. So upset was King Connor at the way Coo-Cullen was being treated that he went off to Scotland on a visit, leaving Coo-Cullen, who hadn't the heart to go, alone, among the hostile people of Ulster.

The occasion was just the one that Queen Maeve had been expecting. No sooner had King Connor left Ulster's shore than she marched her army against Ulster. Her huge array soon disposed of the champions that King Connor had left at the passes into Ulster, and before the women and children of Ulster had a chance to look around they were at the mercy of her cruel soldiers. Coo-Cullen, as usual, because of the whispering campaign, was away in quiet places. One night he saw a glow in the sky near his mother's house, so, all unwitting, he drove across in his chariot to see what was going on. He just got there in time to see his mother's house burning to the ground, and his dear mother being dragged along by her hair to become a slave to Queen Maeve. Men never knew what happened to that raiding party of Queen Maeve. A few bits and pieces of them floated down a few weeks later, but the sight of his mother being dragged along threw Coo-Cullen into such a frenzy that he never knew what he did to those men. He must have chopped them up into little pieces, and then, putting his mother in a safe place, he rode against the whole army of Ireland. The Ulster people, when they saw him riding past, forgot all the old vicious stories about him, and blessed him as he stormed past them in a cloud of dust. Coo-Cullen was become again the Hound of Ulster. Some of them, with more sense, caught a boat for Scotland, to tell King Connor what was going on, and all the while Coo-Cullen held off the army of Queen Maeve.

He did not challenge them to single combat this time, because he could no longer trust the word of the Queen, but all night and day he hovered and worried their flanks, worrying them and killing the sluggards, just like the hound he was. His harassing tactics however could not completely hold up the army of Queen Maeve, which daily inched further and further into Ulster. At length Coo-Cullen could allow them to go no further, for right in front of the advancing army the women had taken refuge with their children, and Coo-Cullen knew what would happen to them if once Queen Maeve got hold of them. So one fine morning in September the army saw Coo-Cullen, fully dressed as a warrior, in his chariot, his driver beside him, standing right in the path. Coo-Cullen was at bay for Ulster, and a long sigh went up from the Irish host, for they knew that many of them would die that day.

Coo-Cullen was out of range of the blowpipes. Moreover a strong breeze was blowing his battle standard straight out from its pole, so Queen Maeve sent her cavalry against him. Just like in his first fight, against the boys of the King's House, Coo-Cullen had cunningly chosen his ground, where the path was narrow, between two high hills, so that only about five of the Irish cavalry could come against him at one time. All day long he slaughtered them, until his arm grew tired, and the pass was littered with the corpses and the carcasses of the Irish and their horses. It was a hunter's moon that night, so the fight went on after dark, and by dawn Coo-Cullen could hardly be seen across the mound of dead as the Irish infantry clambered over them after him. At last a blowpiper got within range, and let Coo-Cullen have it, right between the eyes.

A moment later his driver was wounded with a spear, and he turned on Coo-Cullen and said: "That is the first time, Hound, that you have let a spear past you to hit me."

Coo-Cullen smiled as well as he could and said: "It didn't get past me, my heart of corn, it went through me." And so it had.

The end was near, and King Connor still far away. As the driver lay dying, Coo-Cullen staggered to a tree, and tied himself so that he could not fall, and faced the enemy that way. Although he was near to his death from his gaping wounds, and from the poison, none of the Irish dared approach him all that day and the next, and Coo-Cullen glared at them, grasping his sword and spear, until, from afar off he heard the skirl of King Connor's army coming. Queen Maeve stood on the mound of dead, and stared at Coo-Cullen closely, leaning up against the tree. Then she started, and with a wild shout she ran toward Coo-Cullen, for her sharp and beady eyes had noticed at the hero's feet was a badger drinking Coo-Cullen's dripping blood, while overhead a vulture was circling easily, with all the time in the world to spare. The Irishmen followed her, and crowded around the dying hero, watching him die.

Coo-Cullen cared not at all. He knew Ulster was safe now, and that his time had come. He undid the rope that bound him to the tree, and, on hands and knees, because there was no strength in him, he crawled amid the feet of the silent staring Irish, and lifted a water bottle off one of the men he had killed. He lifted it shakingly to his mouth and drank and sighed deeply. Then he looked straight through the baffled Queen Maeve and smiled and died, going to join the other soldiers of all ages and climes in the queer limbo of Fiddlers' Green, where those men go who have fought the good fight, but have only known the joy of battle and have never seen the splendor of the Rising Son of God.

# X

# THE GIANT FINN MACCOOL

SOMEHOW it's only after a job is done that they find out the easy way to do it. There are steam shovels and bulldozers now, but when they were building the roads across America there were none of these things. There were only men. It was men who built the roads that went snaking westward; it was men who laid the ties and drove the spikes, and many a one of them, as he sweated and grunted and heaved, thought back with longing of the land he'd left behind him. There were lots of Irish in the railroad gangs and, big and tough as they were, they would never have achieved their high estate as princes of the pick and shovel brigade if it had not been for their champion, the creature Finn MacCool.

Finn had been helping the Irish with their problems from 'way back. When they wanted to cross over to Scotland to settle an argument he threw rocks in the sea for them to use as a causeway, and many a weary sailor has cursed Finn MacCool ever since for his well-intentioned stone-throwing. Most of the rocks are still standing up out of the ocean, and the gulls scream and circle above them as the ships cautiously tiptoe around the jagged, worn-down, steppingstones.

Finn was never very bright, but he was willing, God help him. He was such a big man himself that he thought big, so that if a distressed Irishman called on him for help he generally got loaded down with far too much of whatever it was he had been wanting. If a tired farmer called on Finn to dig him a ditch Finn would dig one so wide and deep that the whole of the farmer's land would be shoveled under the muck that Finn threw over his shoulder in his digging, and the ditch itself would be so deep that anybody falling into it would have time to holler for Finn to come and lift him out before he hit the bottom. Finn was such a clumsy man as well as being so almighty strong. Whenever the children of Ireland were in bed, which is always good and early in that proper land, Finn would walk through Ireland as quietly as he could, and he would be so intent upon his walking that he would never notice where he was going. He stepped on Dublin Castle that way once, and the place has never been the same since. Of course, the Castle people blamed the rebel men for flattening it, and there has always been great argument as to who really was to blame. The rebel men were so pleased at being imagined so strong by the Castle people that they never owned up that on that very night they were all plotting in Dolan's bar, and Finn was so high up that he never even noticed that the Castle was looking rather lower down than usual.

For all Finn's clumsiness the Irish people have always liked him. They are rather proud of him in a way, because there are not many nations these days that have their own giant. Still and all, they were glad when he went to America, where it's so big that he's hardly noticed.

Finn had heard of America ever since St. Brendan had discovered it about a thousand years before Columbus hit the shore. St. Brendan always said that he wished that he had stayed on over there, but when he met the Indian tribe of Micmacs he thought that they were the queerest looking Irishmen that he had ever seen, so he went back to the Old Country, where he told everybody about the Micks that he had met with feathers in their hair. Finn knew about America all right, but although he stepped across once or twice he didn't like the looks of it. There was too much hustle and bustle there for Finn, who used to like to stretch out along the top of a range of hills and watch the fishing boats put in to Galway Bay. Ireland suited Finn fine, as long as there were plenty of people to talk to, but, about a hundred years ago Finn noticed that there were fewer and fewer of his friends around, and that hundreds of boats were heading always for America. One day Finn saw a swank young lad hurrying on his way to Cork harbor with his bundle on his shoulder, so Finn picked him up between his thumb and forefinger and asked him what the score was. He had to hold the lad very close to his ear to get the answer, for to Finn a human voice was only about as loud as a bat's squeak.

"Haven't you heard, Finn, my decent fellow," said the young Irishman, "that all the young people of Ireland are off to the green fields of America? Sure the streets are paved with gold over there, and there is hardly a potato in the whole wide expanse of the country. It's meat and milk and butter that the people live on over there, and it's away from the English, so we are all for off. Put me down now, my heart of corn, or I'll be missing the boat that is straining to get away from the harbor yonder."

Finn put young Owen Downey on his feet again gently, "God bless you, Owen lad," said he, "may God be with you every foot of the way you take"; but Finn said it absent-mindedly, because he had been to America. He'd leaned over Boston anyway, and he had seen no streets paved with gold. He also thought he had seen something else, but he hadn't; he had only had a bad dream about a place that was to grow up later, called Pittsburgh. Finn thought that America was a queer place for the Irish to be wanting. They were never a very energetic people if there was any money in it, and as far as he could see, that was the main thing about America; the people he had seen had all hustled after money. "Still," he rubbed his head, "I'm the biggest and thickest Mick that ever was or will be, so I guess I saw the wrong America."

The years went by until there were no young folk left in Ireland at all. Finn used to miss the music of the crossroads' dances, and the skirl of the pipes was now very quavering as an old man played them, or taught the skill of it to a wee lad who was waiting to go on the next boat to America. Finn liked the old folks and the children very much, but he was never like the children and he would never be like the old folk, because giants come in only one size, and they stay that way, being creatures. One fine, quiet, soft day Finn took a turn across Connemara, which was his favorite stamping ground, it being hardly settled at all, and he suddenly realized why he was feeling so restless and so lonesome. "Begad," said he, "I'll step across the water, and see how my friends are getting along over there in America."

Well, when Finn MacCool, hidden in the clouds and wearing his flying boots, hovered over America a great sadness came over him. Most of the poor Irish, not having the fare, had got no further than the Atlantic coast, and they were huddled in poor houses along there, in Boston and New York and such-like places. Finn thought that it was like landing in a lovely country and never getting beyond the grimy water front, for he could see over the Appalachians, and he could see the lovely land that lay beyond. He picked up some of the Irish in his fingers, out of Boston, and they told him that the streets had not been paved with gold at all, and that here they were all stuck in the big city with never a chance of getting out of it.

Finn kept them in his hand while he got to thinking. At last he said: "Well why don't they build a railroad that will open up that lovely Western land?" At that the Irish stared at him. "Is it a railroad? Why man, there are high mountains and muskeg, lakes and rivers so big that you could sink all Ireland in the middle of them and it wouldn't cause a hazard for a passing steamboat. Is it a railroad? Why, they would need supermen to build such a road."

Finn smiled at them. He put them all down except Big Mauler Donovan, and he said to him: "Mauler, go and tell the people with the money that the Irish will put the railroad through for them." Mauler gasped at that, but he saw that Finn had something on his mind, and nobody ever thought of crossing Finn, because he never did any real harm, and he was a gentle man, and decent too, underneath it all. Why, Mauler remembered the last time he had seen Finn. The big giant was baby-sitting for the village of Ballycarty, while the parents and big children had gone to Inchycooly to the circus. Finn had sat on an adjacent hill, and had watched over the town like an old hen watches her chicks. Thinking of things like that, Mauler agreed to go to the monied people. They jumped at the idea, maybe in order to try and put a railroad through or maybe, as some people have suggested, to get the Irish out of Boston.

The Irish took the picks and shovels and went to work. They were issued with barrels of beer and plenty of hamburgers to keep them going, but it was slow and weary work. Finn watched them from above the clouds, and as long as the going was only average tough he stayed watching. When they came up against muskeg he would tell them to lay off for the day, and he would take about fifty shovels and squeeze and stretch them together until he got one big enough to handle. Then, looking like a big buck Irish navvy enlarged about fifty times, he would dig through that muskeg, find the bedrock, tap piles in it with the flat of his shovel, and lay the ties across, that he kept in his mouth, like bobby pins. In a day he would get the rails across the worst stretch of muskeg, and then the Irish would take over again, until they struck another bad patch.

It was when they struck a bad patch, and were resting, that they got the bad name for fighting and causing disturbances all through the West. Until now people have always wondered how they had time to tarryhoot so much when they were laying the rails at such a rate. It was just the same as the time Finn Mac-Cool stepped on Dublin Castle. He never noticed the work, and the Irish were quite flattered to let people think that they did all the incredible labor that went in to the opening up of America. Among themselves the Irish have always given the credit to Finn MacCool, but it's only recently, in our time, that the Irish have got around to talking with any other people except themselves.

One fine day the railroad ran all across America, although you still have to change trains at Chicago. Finn felt fairly happy about the whole thing. The Irish had settled down along the tracks. Some of them even stuck it out at St. Paul. Too many of them stayed in Boston. The Bostonians couldn't get nearly enough of them working on the railroad, and an Indian chief called Tammany had kept a lot of them in New York. Still, Finn had, by his exertions, given all America a leaven of Irish, and because he had done so well by the States he made up his mind to stay there. He has some friends among the wise people, the little creatures of Ireland, and they fixed it so that he looks just like a big Irishman to other people, although he is really as big as he ever was. Sometimes he takes a turn at being Mayor of New York, sometimes he's a cop in Dubuque, Iowa. He just ambles around, visiting his people. The Irish still see him as gigantic as ever, but they don't tell anybody. They don't want to embarrass the big fellow. The last time Mauler Donovan's grandson saw him he was holding back the Germans in the Battle of the Bulge, in the late great war. The Germans, and the other Americans, thought it was just another fighting Irishman, but, of course, it was Finn MacCool.

It's about time the Irish had another heavyweight champion of the world. The Irish have been talking about it for quite a while now. Don't be surprised if a Jerry Driscoll or a Shamus Hennessy starts mowing them down in the preliminaries soon. The only snag with the scheme, say the Irish, is that Finn might come up against another fighter with some Irish in him, and then he would refuse to fight, because the Irish lad would see Finn at his real size, and they wouldn't be able to hit one another — as if Finn would ever hit an Irishman. It's all very difficult, say the Irish, for, as everybody knows, nearly all great heavyweights, barring the colored folk, must have some Irish in them somewhere, or they would never be able to start. For all that, it's very probable that the Irish will work out some way to get Finn to put the gloves on. They weren't ashamed of letting him build the railroad for them, all except for the long easy stretches. Is there any reason to doubt at all that they won't let him win the world's championship for them? They do say that John L. Sullivan was really . . . but's that's another story.

# XI

# THE LEPRECHAUNS

EVERYBODY has heard about the leprechauns, but nobody knows much about them. They are the queer, hidden, little people of Ireland, and for a while it was they who made Ireland the wonder of the world, for while the Irish did their courting and their dancing and their singing it was the leprechauns who did all the work. It's a sad fact that in the old days, not now of course, the Irish would pass up the chance of making a dollar just to see a couple of horses trying to race each other, or a fiddler scraping away at some old tune that a man might be humming for him to copy down with his violin. The rest of the world wondered how it was that the Irish always seemed to have time for all the pleasant things in life, and yet they managed to look well fed and prosperous at the same time. It was called the Golden Age of Ireland, and so it was, for the Irishmen, although the leprechauns were not so sure about it. In their history books, which are written on the bottoms of their shoes, as they think that history has to be rewritten every day anyhow, they refer to this time as the Age of the Captivity, and so it was for the poor, wee creatures.

For those who have never seen a leprechaun it might be just as well at this point to describe one. They are much smaller than is generally supposed. So many actors have tried to play the part of a leprechaun on the stage that they have to make a leprechaun almost as big as a small man, which is silly. A real, live leprechaun is about the same size as a ground squirrel, and he is just about as easy to catch. They are not wrinkled little men at all, but they are just like us in appearance, only about ten times smaller. There are little boy leprechauns as well as old man leprechauns, and the only thing that they all have in common is their great neatness and tidiness in dressing, and their amazing dexterity as shoemakers. They are the greatest shoemakers in the world, although not for human beings of course. They make the shoes for all the good little folk of the world, for the elves of England, and for the gnomes of Europe, and even for the Spang-Los of distant China. If ever an elf or a gnome really wants to feel that he is the best-dressed man in town he has to be wearing a pair of leprechaun shoes. These tiny shoes are made out of tanned mouse skin, and they are as supple and as elegant as a pair of shoes can be. The shoemaking is the leprechauns' pride and joy, but it is also their undoing.

Many years ago, when the leprechauns were as big as ordinary people were in those days, they did some terrible thing. Nobody quite knows what it was, least of all the leprechauns, who don't even know that they were once as big as ordinary people. The old men have it in Ireland that it was something to do with their meanness, for they are the meanest people that have ever been seen. It seems that they were so eager to make money that they worked all the time, and never lifted their eyes even to look at a cloud going by, or to see the coming of spring, or even to compliment a passer-by upon his appearance. All they cared about, as they still do, was making money. They never had time to do a good deed, and they would never think of asking a man if he had a mouth on him on the hottest day of the year. So, as they didn't even notice the glories of the world, nor its joys and sorrows, they were made into little people, and they were allowed to find their only happiness in being neat and clean and punctual and industrious, God help them. To make matters worse, a man only has to catch one of them and hold him tight and turn a deaf ear to the pleas of the little creature, and the leprechaun must yield up to his captor all his savings or do all his work for him the livelong day. They are so small and so agile, just like a squirrel, that they are hard to catch, but they can't help giving themselves away sometimes because of the tap-tap-tap of their little shoemakers' hammers. The tap-tap-tap is very tiny, not as loud as a cricket's chirp, but it can be heard by a man with a keen ear, and maybe that is why the Irish always look as if they were listening for something distant. Have you ever noticed that?

The leprechauns always have their neat, little, underground houses in quiet places, and they always work at night, but sometimes, when there is a hunter's moon, they break surface so that they can work in the light of the moon, and so save candles. That is the only time they can be caught, and it was on a night like that that the Golden Age of Ireland began.

The king of the elves in England had been courting the queen of the gnomes in France, and at long last the match had been arranged. It was going to be such a splendid affair that both the king and the queen placed a contract for hundreds of pairs of shoes with the leprechauns. It was to be a rush job, as the marriage was to take place on Midsummer night, which was only three weeks away, and the leprechauns had to work night and day to be able to finish the shoes and beat the deadline. In order to work better all the little creatures came together from all over Ireland, and they set up a kind of assembly line. The tapping of their wee hammers was so insistent that it sounded more like the steady drum of rain than anything else. Of necessity, because they couldn't help being mean any more than men can help being human, they all came up to work by the light of the moon. They knew that it was taking a chance, but there was a saving to be made, so up they all trooped that fateful night.

Up to that time the Irish had been just like other people. They had to work hard for anything that they possessed, and there was little enough time for sporting, or the long silent conversations, leaning on a gate, looking out over the sea, that are even better than any sporting, even better than horse racing itself. It was especially hard on the Irish, as anybody knows who has ever been to Ireland. It is such a soft and lovely land, with so many attractions, that a man can sit all day and think that he is in heaven itself, whereas in fact all that he is doing is looking between a gap in the hills out on the gray-green Irish sea. The Irish did their best, but they sometimes had to cut their conversations short to gather the hay, and it had been known for a prize fight between the Dublin Slasher and Brian Quinn to be postponed because a thunderstorm began to threaten a standing harvest. The occasional Irishman had caught a leprechaun, but he had never had the heart to insist upon the bargain, and he had always heeded the promises of the squirming little creature that if he was put down he would come back with the money at once. They never did come back, and an Irishman had never had a second chance, because it is only once in a lifetime that a man gets a go at them. Once a lifetime every Irishman has a chance of living fine and easy, but hardly any of them have ever had the hard streak to make the wee people keep their bargain.

Just at this time, however, all the Irish were feeling pretty low. There had been a series of bad harvests, and even the potatoes had given out on them. They had not even been able to fill the children's stockings at the last Christmas, and the way things were looking they might not be able to fill them on the coming one. Moreover it had been the loveliest spring that they ever had seen, and the apple blossoms of Waterford and the cherry blossoms of Antrim were fit for the Queen of Heaven herself. Instead of having time to look at them, and to breathe deep at the lovely air that hung around the orchards, the Irish were kept busy panting trying to keep body and soul together. They were in the mood, in other words, for something that would break the drab monotony of their existence.

It was Rory Sullivan who first noticed the drumming noise of the tapping hammers, when he was taking a walk away from his work, trying to compose a poem praising a girl with soft brown hair. He was a leery man, that same Rory, so he crawled up to the lip of a hollow and looked over the top. A grin of sheer delight broke over his favored face when he saw the whole nation of leprechauns tapping away. He hadn't had his one chance of a lifetime yet, and many was the time that he lay dreaming, thinking of what he would do if he met one of the little people, and now here were the whole lot of the creatures.

Rory quietly let himself slide down from the lip of the hill, and he lay on his back and looked at the moon, thinking up a plan to catch them. He was a poet, and so he had big ideas. At last he had the great idea, and stepping out smartly reached the nearest township and awakened the people with his news. None of them had had their chance at a leprechaun yet, and they listened eagerly to Rory's grand idea. The men with horses mounted them, and within an hour a whole army of people from all around had gathered to help out. Rory led them back to the hill. That man would have been a general in later days, because the way he handled his forces was masterly. The men had brought their fishing nets, and, stationing some of them between the leprechauns and the holes to the tunnels that led to the underground dwellings, the others advanced upon the busily tap-tapping leprechauns.

It was a clean sweep. Every leprechaun in Ireland, which is in all the world, was leaping and squeaking in a net in no time at all. The people would have listened to their heart-rending pleas if it had not been for the bold Rory. He just laughed at them, and he made them a proposition. They could keep their gold, said he, if they would do half the work of all Ireland, so that the Irish could enjoy their days in decent comfort. It wasn't their money he was after, but their beady-eyed industry, that all the Irish lacked above all things. The chief of the leprechauns agreed with a thankful sigh. As long as their money was safe, why, they would work the clock around. And so they did, from that day. Incredible as it may seem, not only did the leprechauns do all the work on the shoemaking business, just as before their capture, but they also did half the work of Ireland. It's incredible, but fairly true, and the Irish lived from that time on in decent enjoyment and in propriety. Well — nearly always in propriety.

That was how the Irish managed to give the appearance of both living and working hard. The leprechauns were doing half their work for them, but the other nations did not know that. The scheme worked for centuries. The leprechauns were used to work, and they wouldn't have enjoyed leisure if they had had it, so the Irish didn't feel too bad about it, and they were able to be the playboys of the Western World.

It was too good to last. One year, not long over an age ago, the Irish bred a jumping horse that they were sure would beat the world, and they put the shirts off their backs on him in their betting. They were so sure that he would win that they even borrowed money off the leprechauns to bet upon that leaping marvel of a horse — and he was beaten by an English horse called Idiot's Delight, at Aintree, in England.

Of course, the Irish could not pay the leprechauns back, so the little folk got their freedom, and they dashed back to their 100 per cent shoemaking with thin little inhuman cries of delight. The years of enjoyment had given the Irish even more distaste than they had had before for the dreary grind of daily chores, and they sighed with impatience for the good old days of the leprechauns. At last they could stand it no longer. Besides, the leprechauns were always making fun of them, so most of them left for the green fields of America, which is where they are now. Some of them go back to Ireland for a holiday, and they always have their ears cocked for the wee tap-tap. The Irish in Ireland swear that not a leprechaun has been seen since the day the jumping horse was beaten, but it's hard to believe that, for how in the name of heaven do those same people seem to get along with so much enjoyment and not a hustle in the whole lot of them?

# XII

## PATRICK WILL TAKE OVER

ST. PATRICK was a gentleman; he came from decent people, but the poor lad was looking after pigs and going to bed hungry when all his friends were having the gay time, and they growing up. It would have been fine if Patrick could have stayed at home in the days of his youth, on the banks of the Severn River, on the borders of lovely Wales. But it was not to be. One fine day some pirates out of Norway sailed up the Severn in their long boat, and they snatched the young lad before the screams of his mother could bring his father to save him. Ever since the Roman soldiers had gone away, the pirates and the Irish were getting bolder and bolder against the poor British people, and young Patrick was strapped to the mast of the long boat and taken over to Ireland, where he was sold as a slave. He, the son of a gentleman — that's what his name means in the Roman language — looked after hogs for ten long years of his life. He grew to manhood always smelling of pig.

Year after year Patrick herded swine for his master, between the high blue hills of Mourne and the gray-green sea. He learned to speak the language of the Irish, which is a fine language for making love or insulting people, but is not much good for exact statement, as is the Latin, which was Patrick's native tongue. In short, Irish is a very proper language for the Irish people, and it was necessary in those days to have the Irish at you before they could understand a word that was said.

It's all different now, of course. The Irish speak English better than the English do themselves, so the Irish say, and what's the use of contradicting them?

His Irish master, in his own queer way, was kind enough to young Patrick, but the master was so fond of his hogs that he used to get a bit testy with Patrick for always casting a yearning look out across the sea, to where he had known home and happiness. One day, when Patrick was quite a young man, his master told him to clear the hell out, because the pigs, he thought, had begun to sense that Patrick would have preferred to have been some place else. Patrick took his freedom joyfully, before the man could change his mind, and he managed to get a passage on an Irish ship that was going across the sea on its monthly trip to harass Hereford or to burn down Barnstaple. When he got to where his home had been, all that Patrick could find was a blackened ruin, like the stumps of old trees, where his lovely home had sat. It was a time of great desolation in Britain. Patrick never was to see his mother and father again. He turned sadly away from Britain, where he had been born, and sailed across the sea to France, where he knew that his Uncle Martin would be able to help him.

Uncle Martin loved the fine, tall young man who looked so much like his dear father, who had been Martin's brother. He fitted him out with clothes and gave him a home while Patrick caught up on his education, which had been sadly neglected in Ireland. Soon Patrick stopped smelling even faintly of pig and he began to be regarded by people as a coming young man. Now in those days the Church was only really starting and since the Roman Empire had fallen there was great need of able men to serve the Roman Church, to keep order, and to teach reading and writing.

Patrick wanted to share in the making of the new Church, so he became a priest and in no time at all he was a bishop. That should have satisfied any man, but Patrick felt all the time that he was lacking something. He couldn't sleep or eat very well, and always in his dreams he heard a crowd of people imploring him for something in a strange language. Then, one night, when he was fully trained as a churchman and was still young enough to be healthy, he had the dream more clearly than ever before, and this time he woke up with a shock, for the people were speaking quite clear and loud to him.

"Patrick," they were saying, "Patrick, come back to Erin."

He had forgotten that the Irish was at him all the time he was studying and preparing, and it seemed to come back to him that very night. With that Patrick went straight to the Pope.

"Holy Father," said he, for Patrick was never one to make fancy speeches, "Holy Father, I'm off for Ireland. Fare you well."

"Wait now, Patrick, wait now, son," said the Pope anxiously. "Sure you don't want to go to Ireland. If it's heathen that you want to convert why don't you go, with my blessing, to the jungles of darkest Africa, where at least you'll have a sporting chance. But to go to Ireland! Why, lad, they make stew out of Christians and roasts out of British bishops. You'll never convert those boys."

"Still, Holy Father, I'm going. Good-by now." With that Patrick marched out of the Pope's room and packed his bundle. He was just for off when the Pope caught him.

"Good-by, Patrick, little son," said the Pope. "I was a foolish, scared, old man in there. If I were younger I'd be with you myself. I have sent a call for volunteers to go with you, and the boys are getting ready to join you now. Old Captain Jonas is going to land you there from his ship, in the middle of the night. He says it's taking a chance going up there, but he'll do it for me. So there you are, Patrick — is there anything else that I can do for you?"

"No, Holy Father," said Patrick gently, "except to give me your blessing." So the old Pope gave the young man his blessing and off went Patrick with a high heart to climb aboard the ship of Captain Jonas that was to take him to the land of his dreams. His volunteer help were all fine young men, more anxious to see famous Ireland than anything else. A week or so later, it doesn't matter, the boat gently grounded south of Dublin, and Patrick and his companions climbed up the steep cliff to a high place where they could look around.

Now the ground was green and moist, and under their feet there was the squirming and the writhing and the hissing of snakes. Ireland had more snakes to the square inch in those days than the desert has sand; they were the bane of Ireland. To keep them away, as well as to get warm, Patrick got his followers to kindle a huge fire, and Patrick and his people stood around the fire and sang a song to God to thank Him for getting them this far safe.

Just a few miles away, on a hill, O'Leary, the lord of all Ireland, had his camp. One of his pagan wise men woke him and said, "O'Leary, if you don't put yonder fire out tonight, you'll never put it out, man."

At that O'Leary and his soldiers and his priests drove over to Patrick's camp to have a good night's sport burning the strangers. When they got there, with all their screaming, they didn't find a pack of frightened wretches trying to hide, but they found Patrick and his men standing up straight and waiting for them.

"It is O'Leary, isn't it?" asked Patrick courteously. He was always the gentleman, was Patrick.

O'Leary nearly fell out of his chariot when he heard this noble stranger address him in Irish. He turned and looked at his wise men to know the way of it, but they just looked wise and said nothing. O'Leary felt less disposed to burn a fellow Irishman than he did a foreigner, so the poor man all innocently asked Patrick what he was after in Ireland.

Patrick was always the great preacher. He had a lovely flow of words when he wanted them, and this night he nearly blew the Irish over with his eloquence. He told them of the Birth in a stable at Bethlehem, and straightway O'Leary wanted the Baby to come back to earth, and this time to try in Ireland, "where, with all our faults, God help us," said O'Leary, "we'd always find a place for the Little Fellow."

Patrick could hardly keep from smiling when he thought of our Lord with twelve Irish apostles, but he sternly told O'Leary to shut up, and he went on with the story of how God had come down to earth. When he had finished the story of the Crucifixion even he himself was crying, and O'Leary and his tribesmen were sobbing. If Patrick had stopped there he could have baptized them all at once, for they all wanted to be followers of such a Man as Patrick had told them about. But Patrick was an honest man, and he went on then to tell of God the Father and God the Holy Ghost who were also God, but were different persons at the same time.

O'Leary scratched his head at that, and looked sideways at his wise men, who had begun to smile, seeing that Patrick had struck a snag with this new teaching. So Patrick tried to tell the doctrine of the Trinity more slowly to O'Leary and his clan, but O'Leary still scratched his head and couldn't get it. At last Patrick lost his temper with them, all in the firelight on the marshy green of that snake-ridden land.

"Why, you stupid omadhaum," he roared, "you walking on

three in one all the time here in Ireland, and you, you big thick Mick, you can't see it!" And with that Patrick bent down and plucked a sprig of shamrock, which only grows in Ireland — everywhere else they call it clover — and showed O'Leary the three wee leaves on the one stem, the single plant with the three parts. With that a great light dawned on O'Leary and he and all his people became Christians on that hour.

In a few years Patrick had converted all of Ireland, except Ulster maybe, and for the rest of his life he toiled among the Irish, and, like all people who go to live in Ireland, he became more Irish than the Irish themselves.

The older he got the more he worried about the Irish, and about what would happen to them after he had gone on to heaven, so when he knew that he was not long for this world he went off on his own to a high mountain, that is called Patrick's Hill to this day. There he fasted and prayed for Ireland for all of thirty-nine days, and he became sick and faint when he saw the sorrows and tribulations that lay ahead for his dear people in the years that were to come before God would fold up the world for good and all.

He was getting feeble and pale with all his fasting when at last he heard a rustle of wings and saw the heavenly body of the angel that he had been waiting for. It was Gabriel, God's messenger, who came to Patrick.

"Well, Patrick," said the angel in a friendly easy tone, "and God wants to know what you are after, an old man like you, fasting up here in the cold on this high place. God wants to know what you want. He knows that what you want will be for those Irish, and between me and you, Patrick," said Gabriel confidentially, "I'll think you'll be getting what you will be asking for. The Man above has a high opinion of you, Irishman."

So Patrick got up off his weary old knees and wiped the dew from his face and without even saying a salutation to Gabriel he said: "First, let there be no more snakes in Ireland. There's the plague of this green and pleasant land."

Gabriel grinned. "I knew you'd be asking that Patrick, and it's granted." With a swish and a slither every snake left Ireland from that moment and they haven't been seen there since, and that's a solid fact.

"Then," said Patrick, "I'd like God in heaven, my own dear Father, to grant that the Irish will always keep the Faith. God help them, they are going to lose everything else. At least let them cling to that."

Gabriel nodded. "God the Son said that you'd be asking that, and the whole Trinity of Them agreed that you'd earned it. The Irish will always keep the Faith, that's promised."

Then Patrick swallowed hard and looked straight at Gabriel and said without batting an eyelash: "And third, I'd like God, the Father, the Son, and the Holy Ghost, to promise that at the Last Day I'll judge the Irish."

Gabriel would have fallen over backward if it wasn't for his wings. "Mother in Heaven, Patrick. What's this you're asking? Sure you know there isn't a chance of getting that, man."

Patrick, without a word, creaked slowly down on his knees and dourly said: "Get you about your business, errand boy. I'll fast on here until you bring the answer." Gabriel looked at the set of Patrick's face, and without a word flew back to heaven with Patrick's request.

There was consternation up there when They heard about what the stubborn old man was asking for his people. Hours passed and the decision had not yet been reached, when God the Son, who had become Man, said: "Father, let Us give it to Patrick. Sure he is an old and tired man in Our service, and who knows, amid the pleasures of heaven, where he is coming soon, he may forget about the Irish in his enjoyment." The Holy Ghost added His pleading to that of God the Son, because He knew courage when He saw it, and Patrick was all courage where his people were concerned. Besides, God the Son had fasted forty days, and here was this frail old man nearly equaling that. So the Godhead agreed, and Patrick got off his knees with a feeling of great peace and contentment, and went down among his people to prepare for his dying.

Then Patrick died, if such a man can ever die, for wherever there is an Irishman's home, anywhere in the world, there is a Patrick around, driving his mother crazy maybe with his goings on, but somehow, even if it's only in youth, there's some of the real Patrick about the place. Heaven was all set out for the old Patrick and a fine time he had of it, enjoying God and talking to his friends, like Francis, the little Italian, who always had a bird perched on his shoulder, or a wee kitten in his arms, and enjoying fine disputations with Thomas More and the other few lawyers who had managed to get there. Every so often, however, in the midst of his pleasures, Patrick would peep over and see Ireland enduring, and he would be as sad as a saint can be in the green fields of heaven, that are like the pleasant places of Ireland, without the rain.

One day Patrick looked up from his musing to notice that everything was quiet, instead of full of happy bustle, which is usually the way of it up there. He knew somehow that it was the Last Day, and that the Judging had started. He sped along to the Judgment Seat, and he got there just in time. God was just summing up on the Irish, and the list of their charges was nearly as long as His arm. Everybody had a bad word to say for the Irish, and their friends were few, because somehow the Irish never seemed to get on a winning side, and their drinking habits had become notorious and their brawlings and, worst of all, their politics.

The Irish took it all with their heads bowed. God was just getting into His stride when there was a tug at His sleeve, and there was His Patrick, scared, but firm. "You promised, God," said Patrick faintly. God looked at him sternly for a minute, and then He smiled: "If the Irish have earned such love, Patrick, they are worth saving." And He stepped down from the Judgment Seat and Patrick took his place. He tried to look sternly at the Irish, but his love for his foolish people brimmed out of his eyes. The silence made the Irish nation lift their heads, and instead of an infinitely just God, they saw that Patrick, their own darling, whose picture is on walls in homes from Connemara to Wisconsin, was trying to judge them. Patrick, who could be so stern with them when he was alive amongst them, just couldn't say a thing. Tears ran down his cheeks and the Irish were all crying silently too. They all looked so shabby and faithful, the cops, the soldiers with their gaping wounds, and the mothers, so worn down with trying to raise a family decently in tenements in Chicago, they were all there, and Patrick loved them all. The Irish who had given up were not there, although they had generally been far more successful than these beaten people, but somehow the meat packers and the politicians had preferred to be judged with their own social set.

After Patrick had vainly tried to say something for about five minutes, Prince Jesus took him by the arm and gently placed him at the head of the Irish nation, and with Jesus on one side of him and Mary the Mother on the other, St. Patrick led his people into everlasting happiness.

# XIII

## MOTHERS' MEETING

FATHER WALMER made a mouth of bitter tasting whenever he thought of the afternoon that was in front of him. Ever since he had made this parish, out on the mud-flat moors, his Monday afternoon with the mothers had been one of his great rewards. They were not associated with the Union of Catholic Mothers nor with the Catholic Women's League; they were just the parish mothers, and that suited them fine, and it suited Father Walmer fine. They were not the joining sort, neither the priest nor the women, and they liked their independence. Whenever Father Walmer had to go to a Cathedral House meeting he was ill at ease, and as soon as it was over he would hurry back to his beloved parish, the parish of his making, St. Urban on the Moors. It was a self-contained community, on the wrong side of the river, so that it was separate from the major part of town. The people who lived there were the lesser people, mainly dockers and steelworkers who lived in company houses; they were Catholic almost to a man.

Father Walmer loved his people, and they loved Father Walmer. It was surprising, because the priest was an English gentleman, a convert Anglican clergyman, while the parishioners were second-generation Irish, and Father Walmer had only been sent there in order to put a damper on their Irish nationalism, which was flaming in most Catholic seaport parishes of England and Wales during the first quarter of this present century.

The gentle English priest had not curbed them at all. He just loved them in spite of it, the way he loved them in spite of their drinking, in spite of their occasional clashes with the Law, in spite of almost everything about them. They were ignorant, casual, and bedeviling, but they loved God. They built a church, they built a school; they took their religion as naturally and more frequently than they took a bath. They were as remote from Father Walmer's background as could be, and that was the way he liked it. It was his parish, they were his mothers. And now the authorities were trying to spoil it, to organize the mothers into a unit of a central league, and there was nothing that he could do about it. The Honorable Mrs. Lunt-Baugh was coming down from London, with the Cardinal's approval, to organize the parish meetings of the mothers into a federated society.

"Yerra," muttered Father Walmer. He had picked up some of his talking from the mothers, "Yerra, what does the old windbag want coming down here for? Isn't there plenty for her to do in other places without bothering us? These converts. . . ." Father Walmer never thought of himself as a convert. Mrs. Honorable what's her name was to address the parish mothers on this Monday afternoon. Monsignor Colman was going to bring her down to the parish hall for it, and Father Walmer was sure it was going to spoil the whole of all his happy Mondays, from this time on.

At three o'clock Father Walmer wandered across unhappily to the mothers' meeting. They could be heard half a block away, because they had all their preschool children with them, and just as Father Walmer was approaching they were drowning out the bawling of the babies with their spirited rendition of "Sweet Heart of Jesus, Fount of Love and Mercy." They always started the meeting with that hymn; it never varied, just as they always closed with "Soul of My Saviour." As Father Walmer entered the hall Mrs. Donovan, the pianist, had played the last verse of the hymn and had swung into her tea-time music, which was generally excerpts from the "Merry Widow" or the "Desert Song," and the mothers were crowding around the steaming urn of tea and picking up a sticky, sugary bun at the same time, before returning to their seats, which were spaced all around the walls, because there was to be a dance in aid of the football club that evening, and the hall had been readied for it.

Mrs. Duane looked up from counting out the twopences that the mothers were clinking into a basin as they got their tea and buns, and called out delightedly:

"Good afternoon, Father. How are you today? When is this old London blatherskite due to arrive?"

Father Walmer, in his humility, could never get over the fact that all his people were always so delighted to see him. He never saw himself as he was, a tired, shabby, worn-out priest of a working-class parish, a priest who had given all his life to his people. But the people saw it; he was their heart's blood. They knew, although Father Walmer never knew that they knew, that time and time again he had turned down the offers of wealthier, more genteel parishes from the Bishop, and had turned them down in amazement that the Bishop could think that a priest could ever want for a better parish than St. Urban's. The people knew, when the men were on strike, where the money came from that St. Vincent de Paul brothers had distributed for groceries. They knew who put Jerry Dolan through Oxford University, and they knew that Father Walmer would still be wearing his ragged overcoat if Sullivan the publican had not slipped it out of the sacristy one night and got Coghlan the tailor to run up an Irish frieze one from its shape. Whenever anybody gave Father Walmer the money to buy new clothes he always slipped it to the poor. He loved the poor, and as the whole parish was poor, they all loved him. The people knew, although Father Walmer never knew, that the Bishop had even told the Pope about his brother priest. If the St. Urban's mothers are to be believed the Holy Father slapped his head, the way Gazzi the fishmonger used to when he was excited, and said to the Bishop: "You are lucky, son Michael, to know such a one." But the mothers always volubly exaggerate; maybe the Pope never smacked his head at all.

Father Walmer looked around the hall, seeking out his favorite corner. There they were, the great mothers. There was Lizzie Desmond and Nora Hart, Mary Ann Sullivan and Kate Burke. He made his way over to them, stepping over the battling, playing, squalling children. The place was a pleasant bedlam, with the clatter of the teacups, the high laughs of the women breaking out over their shrill conversation, and the banging away on the piano of the hammer-handed Mrs. Donovan.

As Father Walmer neared his corner he thought once again about his favorite topic — the mothers. He felt humble in front of them. Every morning at Mass there would be fifty or sixty of them, following the Mass with their rosary beads wrapped around their fingers, with their lips moving in the beloved prayer to Mary. He could never get them to become daily communicants — in their ignorance they thought that they were not good enough — but once a month all the mothers would leave their Dinnys and their Josephs, their Parks and their Jims, probably nursing a hang-over, at home with the children of a Sunday morning and they would congregate for their Communion Mass. And God, Father Walmer felt sure, never found a better home than in the hearts of those mothers.

Next Thursday was the annual outing of the mothers. Most of them had no idea where it was going to. Oxford or Ballsbridge — what did it matter? It was their annual Bacchanalia, and the butchers and the grocers, the insurance men and the rent collectors, the Johnny Fortnights who came around collecting for the clothes they had supplied always resignedly crossed that week off their lists. The mothers used to charter a bus, start off bright and early, singing and laughing like little girls, for one blessed day leaving all their troubles behind them. The bus would career through the green countryside, and the driver, whom they all called "son" and who called them all "Ma," would pull up discreetly at some quiet country inn, at the first opportunity, and in all the mothers would troop, giggling and nudging one another for their festival drink — port wine mixed with lemonade — while Father Walmer and the driver would sit on the running board of the bus, smoking their pipes and enjoying the day.

There would always be a few stops before the destination, which was always some holiday town, like Stratford-on-Avon or Leamington, anywhere where there was a good lunch served, and the liquor laws were easy. As soon as they got there Father Walmer would leave them to it. He would wander off, lunch quietly on his own, and thoroughly enjoy the day, getting back to the bus about half an hour before it was due to start, and would quietly organize the return trip. It needed organizing, for by this time the mothers had got quite a few ports and lemons inside of them, and were prone to break into a jig in the main street or let off steam in some exhibition or other.

Father Walmer would never forget, until his dying day, and

maybe he would even remember it past his dying, the time they had last year.

For some reason or other the committee had picked on London for the outing. Most of the mothers had never been to London, nearly fifty miles away, so it was a great event, and the day had started bright and early. Lizzie Drennan had a son in the London Fire Department, so she was the great metropolitan, because of her Vincent's position, and she became the major-domo of the party; but Father Walmer unobtrusively hung around them for a while, just to see the impact that the heart of Empire would make upon St. Urban's mothers.

The bus stopped and disembarked them all at Leicester Square. At once Lizzie started organizing. "This way, girls," she said, and dived across the road, followed by her "girls," whose average age was about forty-five, and the London traffic had to rear back on its heels to let the mothers live. Somehow their holiday spirit even struck the Londoners, because no fulminations emanated from anyone over their fecklessness. Even a London cabby is said to have smiled at them.

Like an arrow Lizzie led them to Westminster Abbey. "This is it, girls," said she. "We haven't got time to pay a visit, so let's all kneel down here and say a decade. Sure, that's better than going in and goggling anyway."

Father Walmer hid himself amid the crowd at that. In front of the great Gothic medieval pile of the Abbey, England's shrine, the mothers matter-of-factedly fell upon their knees and, led by Lizzie, started to say the First Joyful Mystery. The crowd, a London crowd, on a bustling Thursday morning, a sophisticated, tough crowd, just couldn't pass this by. Before the mothers had got up to the third Hail Mary there was such a crowd that the street was blocked. The mothers were quite unaware of the people milling around them, until a policeman shouldered his way through the crowd and tapped Lizzie on the shoulder.

Lizzie looked up and said, "Go away, son, can't you see we are saying the rosary? Go away, there's a good boy." And on went Lizzie into the first part of the fourth Hail Mary. "But Ma," the policeman interrupted, "sure you've got the wrong church. Westminster Abbey is the Protestant building."

Lizzie looked at him unbelieving for a second, her lips still moving in prayer, then, when she saw that he kicked with the right foot and was no old codder she leaped to her feet dramatically, arms outspread. "Stop!" she cried, "Stop, mothers, this here is the bloody Protestant place." The mothers cut off their rosary so fast their teeth clicked. Lizzie was horrified and repentant. "Girls," she said, "I wouldn't have had this happen for anything." Turning to the policeman she said, "How do we get to the Cathedral, son?" "Here, Ma," said her policeman, "I'll show you. Begod it's not every day I get to see a sight like I've seen today. So come along now, my beat can look after itself for an hour," and the guardian of the Law led the mothers across the city of Westminster, the old great London, to the brick-red Romanesque pile of the Cathedral.

In the mothers went. Up to the roof they ascended in the elevator, and looked out over London. "Yerra," said they wisely, "sure the Cardinal was a right smart man to let the Protestants keep the old Abbey. Sure this is much more modern."

They had had enough of church by that time, so they made their way to their ordered luncheon, which was in one of those huge and flashy Babylon Hotels that, all decked out in garish trickery, used to glitter all over London before the war.

Lizzie had arranged it well. They had half an hour or more in the cocktail lounge before lunch started. They really loved it, the fizzy new drinks, the banter with the waiters, who were Italians and understood them. It was a lovely time. Such a good time were they having that Father Walmer could not resist it, and came out from behind a potted palm, to be greeted by a chorus of delight. He called for a sherry, which all the mothers insisted on paying for, and the problem was only solved by one of the waiters graciously donating it, and by Father Walmer as graciously accepting it.

Tomorrow the mothers would be back at their washtubs, back to the gray days, but they savored every moment of this day of escape, and Father Walmer offered it up to God for them. Their blitheness was the result of labor, the holy and never-ending labor of bringing up a family. In that cocktail lounge, with all its meretricious glitter, the mothers cast almost a holy glow around the place as they so genteelly sipped at their fancy drinks and giggled at one another over the glasses. Soon, too soon, it was time to eat. They all wended their way to their reserved dining room, shouting back witticisms and thanks to the waiters, and the place was cheap and nasty again.

Liz Nunan and Marg Hayes fell out of line on the way to the dining room. They were two old mothers who had raised their families and, in comfortable circumstances, used to take a daily "wee drop" for the sake of their health. Liz Nunan's son was Johnnie Nunan, the Nonpareil, the great lightweight champion, and he had been a good son to his mother, had Johnnie. None of Liz Nunan's friends ever had to go short, and Liz always had a few sovereigns stashed away for a day like this one. So the two old shawlies dandered back to the cocktail lounge for another quick one, while the luncheon party was settling down. Sure they'd never be noticed missing for five minutes. The pair of them were always dressed in seemly black.

Just as they got to the bar a flashy, greasy city man was buying drinks for a circle of his like acquaintances. The men looked all as wrong as he did, and their women were long-legged painted mates, with long bobs, dyed blonde, and dead laughs, and lovely bodies — which was all they had.

The flashy man was saying to his company, as the two old ones were calling for their drinks, "These Catholic priests. . . . Did you ever notice it? They are always around with women." He muttered an obscenity, just loud enough for his crowd to get, and they laughed their empty laughs, forgetting it, as they forgot everything, as soon as it was said and laughed about.

Liz Nunan and Marg Hayes looked at one another. Liz Nunan tapped the man on the shoulder. His back was toward her. He was holding a brimming cocktail glass in his hand and, as he turned around, Liz, with a flip of her hand knocked the glass up into his face so that the drink splashed straight into it, and the glass broke on his face and cut it. The place went quiet. Liz stood there, quite composed, but with such blazing eyes and such a face of stone that it was certain where the Nonpareil, the matchless, peerless Johnnie Nunan, had come from.

"Don't ever say a thing like that again, son, nor any of you tramps." She took them all in, men and women, with her quiet deadly voice. "Don't ever say a thing like that again. You might get hurt. There might be a man about the place. Never mind the drinks for me and my friend, bartender," Liz said. "This room of yours is full of — things."

The man stayed there, gin and blood running down his face,

the others just kept still. All the rest of the room was looking at them.

"Come on, Marg," said Liz, still white. "We'd better be getting up to the lunch." The two women left. The bartender felt a man again, the first time in years, and as Father Walmer gently chided the two old biddies for being late for lunch, showing that he thought he knew the reason. He did find out the reason later — the bartender told him — but he never let on to Marg and Liz that he knew; it was so much in the pattern of the parish that it seemed quite proper to him.

It was to these women that the Mrs. Honorable was going to come to lecture. Just as he was beginning to brood over it again there was a stir at the door, and in she came, a tweedy Juno, who looked around as if she was visiting her villagers. She really thought that they were her good women. Father Walmer wouldn't have traded the most idle of his mothers — and some of them were idle — for six like her.

He got up wearily and went across to welcome her. She was very businesslike, with her notes and papers, and eager like a beaver to get started talking.

Father Walmer introduced her from the stage, where the band would be playing that night for the dance. She immediately went into her tirade, the usual one of the converts, about England having been the Dowry of Mary, and now the Faith had become an alien thing. She meant *Irish* but was tactful enough to say alien.

Of course the Church in England was alien, Father Walmer said pettishly to himself. The English had lost the Faith, and all the shining knowledge of Newman and all the charity of Chesterton could never replace the people who had wandered away, into their sects and ethics. The Irish had brought the

Faith back. Proudly, yet humbly, they had brought the living God back to his country. There would be few lamps burning in front of the Real Presence in his land were it not for the Irish. The churches were Irish, sure they were Irish. They lacked the form and the pattern of an educated Catholicism, they were vulgar and slipshod often in their liturgy, and often there was not a soul in the parish who would use a missal. Still, the church was crowded, and there was such a love of God that he had seen men weep quietly at the Elevation, men who would hit a man as soon as look at him. His mothers would fall on their knees and pray in the streets of London, and do it as naturally as if they were in their own church. They would smite the enemy without even counting the consequences. They had a love of life, they laughed and sang in this vale of tears, knowing the transience of earth. What did this woman have to come here for?

He listened. It was as bad as he had expected. Mrs. Lunt-Baugh was suggesting to the mothers that they capture the spirit of Merrie England by rigging up a maypole in the parish hall, and dancing around it on their Monday afternoons. She suggested that they take up weaving and spinning, to offset the evils of the factory system. She sounded crazy to the mothers, but they kept their eyes sideways on Father Walmer. They endured her with the passivity of the poor, and with the easiness of not understanding her.

She finished, and she went away. Blank forms came to the presbytery the next day, and Father Walmer filled them in, and Mrs. Duane and Mrs. Farren signed them as secretary and president of the National Sodality. They even got a maypole, which mouldered in the corner of the parish hall. Father Walmer found, to his relief, that the National Sodality made no difference at all. It only meant that Mrs. Duane and Mrs.

Farren hurried back home from meetings in the Cathedral House with the same sense of relief that Father Walmer had been feeling for years, as he crossed back over the bridge to the mud flats, to Urban's on the Moors, to his people, to the parish of his making.

# XIV

## THE IRISH AND THE JEWS AND EVERYBODY ELSE

IN THE window of every house in Ireland on the night before Christmas a candle is burning, and before the people go off to the Church a meal is set on the table and the door is left unlatched. It was not always so, to the everlasting sorrow of the Irish, and to their shame. With their delicate perception they should have known what would happen somewhere, every Christmas Eve, and it always will happen on that night, as long as men are left to live. Every man living has a chance sometime to ease the burden of the Son of God, but generally they do too little, or they do it too late. They would not be men if it were otherwise.

Hundreds and hundreds of years ago the people of Ireland were carefree and gay in their own land. From across the seas people had come to harass them, but the invaders had liked Ireland so much that they had stayed on for the hunting and the fishing, and before they knew what had happened they had begun to call the Irish by their first names; and in time it got so that it was impossible to tell the difference between them and the local people. It was that way that the Irish got their red hair, and their partiality for strong drinking. It was the Viking raiders who came to raid and stayed to settle that brought those two tribulations. The Normans came to conquer

Ireland for the English king, but in no time at all the same Normans were the biggest rebels that the English king had upon his hands. It was only when the English came that the real trouble started.

The great shame that came on Ireland happened before the English came, so the English cannot be blamed for it. The time was one of great prosperity, and all day the people had come in from the adjacent countrysides to go to church at midnight, and to start the Christmas celebrations. There was plenty of money about, and it was flowing freely.

One of the liveliest towns in Ireland at this time was the town of Bundogan, and it was a joy to walk down the main street there on the day before Christmas. A light snow was falling, which is unusual for Ireland, and this added to the festivity of the season, and blotted out the daily noises, so that altogether there was an other-worldly atmosphere about the place. The shops were all glowing with lights, and there were good things for all the family. The children were gazing wide eyed and enchanted at the God's plenty of toys that were to be had at this blessed time, and fat geese and turkeys were hanging up in the butcher shop almost pleading to be basted. Through the gently falling snow friends were hailing one another with "God bless the day," and "A happy Christmas to you!" It was altogether pleasant in Bundogan on that Christmas Eve.

Most of the people who lived a fair way out of town had taken rooms at the local inn, and the children were bundled away into bed fine and early so that they would be ready for the long morning-ride home to their Christmas dinner the following day. All the parcels were stacked in the carts that stood outside the stables, and the women went off to chatter with their friends while waiting for the midnight church service,

while the men joined their companions around a glowing fire
of peat in the barroom of the inn. Everything seemed snug,
and everybody seemed happy with themselves. By nine o'clock
that evening the shops were closing down, the nearby villagers
had started for home, and the inn was filled with a noisy and
good-humored crowd of people, who all felt very pleased with
themselves. They had every reason to feel good. The crops had
been bumper crops for years now, and there was a pig or so
fattening in every yard; there was meat and butter and eggs
for everyone, every day. There was even something over to
send to the missions for those benighted places outside of
Ireland.

When everybody was feeling all cozy and comfortable, with
some hours left for conversation and imbibing before it was
time to start filing into church, the door of the inn, which led
into the barroom, opened and a foreign-looking, middle-aged
man stepped in. He stood there for a moment, until he caught
the eye of the innkeeper, who looked at him coldly, the smile
fading from his face, because he knew that no tinker would
come into the bar on Christmas Eve unless he was after
something.

The tinkers of Ireland are something like the gypsies of
other lands, and yet not quite like them. They wander around,
and have no settled home. They are accused of the occasional
thieving that generally occurs when they camp anywhere near
a town. They have a swarthy foreign look about them, and they
are a bold, independent people who keep apart from the rest
of the Irish, if, indeed, the tinkers can be called Irish.

This middle-aged man didn't quite look like a tinker. But
he was no Englishman — there was too much dignity about
him. He might have been a Spaniard was it not for the gentle
look of him. So everybody put him down as some sort of

renegade tinker, who had lost the free ways of his kinfolk.

The landlord came toward him with the set yet absent-minded look that most people adopt when they are dealing with a man who they think is going to ask them for something. So unusual was it for a tinker to come into their festivities, for the tinkers were always a withdrawn sort of people, that all the talking hushed, and the crowd in the barroom all turned and watched the encounter between the innkeeper and the foreign man. There was no ill will in their looking. They were happy themselves, and they weren't caring one way or the other about the tinker. Indeed, if he had started a whining sort of begging they would all have thrown him a coin or so. But the stranger did not look like the mendicant kind.

"Well," said the landlord, standing between the intruder and the rest of the room. "Well, what is it?"

The man said quietly, "I was wondering if you could put us up for the night. I have a young girl outside, and we have traveled far this day. We would dearly love a welcome here."

"Is it a welcome you are wanting, foreign man?" said the landlord. "Good lord, I couldn't find room for another single body this night. Who is this girl you have outside? Is it your wife that you are talking about?"

"No," said the stranger, "she is not exactly my wife, but I am sort of looking after her, and now, in the snow, she feels that the time for her Baby to come is near. We have nowhere to stay, and there is nobody on this earth to whom we can turn. Will you help me, decent man?"

"She's not exactly your wife, and she is expecting a baby? Why don't you go to the tinkers to help you? After all, they are your own folk." The landlord was rather awkward under the gaze of the quiet, bearded stranger.

"The tinkers are not our folk, landlord, any more than you

are. In a way we feel that you are all our folk, none more so than anybody else. Is there no room here then? Well, perhaps there is somebody here who may help us." Turning around to the people in the barroom the stranger said: "Is there any one among you who will help a young girl, and she in her great need? Is there nobody here who will give up room for the stranger, here in Ireland, on the eve of Christmas?" He said it sadly, not urgently, and not getting an answer, he went on: "Well, we must be on our way then. Perhaps somewhere some-one in the world will give help and shelter to the maiden."

With that he left the barroom, and everybody was quiet for a while after he had left. If he had pleaded with them they would have felt better against refusing him, but he had left without another word. All of a sudden the whole assembly got up and crowded to the door, and they saw the stranger going up the main street, now dark and silent under the falling snow. He was walking himself, but on a donkey, sitting sideways because of her heavy load, was the young maiden of whom he had spoken. They looked so inexpressibly sad as they trudged on their homeless way, that the people were embarrassed and awkward as they slowly went back into the barroom. It was a few minutes before the realization came to them that they had refused shelter to the mother who was about to bear the Child, and then they rushed out pell-mell, silently, desperately seeking to amend. It was too late. The tracks of the Holy Family had been wiped out by the falling snow, and they had gone on someplace else to ask for charity.

Every Christmas St. Joseph and the Blessed Virgin try again their bitter search for a room. Somewhere in the world every day someone in the likeness of God seeks for charity, but because he is poor and is in such need of it he rarely receives it.

And ever since that Christmas night the people of Ireland have tried to make amends for the callous company of Bundogan. In the kitchen of every house in Ireland on the night before Christmas a meal is set on the table, and the door is left unlatched. The Irish are a fair people, and they don't blame the Bundogan folk overmuch for their shame. They know that on some day every town in Ireland, every town in the world has had a chance to take in the Stranger. To blame the people of Bundogan, they knew, was only about as just as blaming the Bethlehem people, or any other people, for that matter.

# XV

# A COAT FOR ST. PATRICK'S DAY

DAN FURLONG, every morning until the children were grown, would wake up around five o'clock and wonder what time it was. The entire household was quite incapable of maintaining a clock in good punctuality. Within a week every clock that they ever obtained would become a liar, so that Dan would miss a shift of work as a result, or the children would be late for school, or Monsignor Phelan would have to talk back to himself at Mass, because his altar boy, Jerry Furlong, had trusted a clock and so was not at the side altar to serve him. Right and left and fore and aft of the Furlongs there were clocks and watches ticking away with monotonous regularity, but somehow they all broke step when the Furlongs got a hold of any of them, so it was to hell with timepieces in that household. Not one of the family would have trusted the sundial in the Vatican gardens, and small blame to them.

Every morning, then, around five o'clock, Dan Furlong would lie awake blinking at the dim ceiling, wondering whether he was early or late or just right. The few warm waking minutes were a great delight to Dan, as they are to most men, and he used to ponder in them. Since the last St. Patrick's Day, when he had worn his herringbone coat, and his companion the Usher had worn his Irish frieze, their sartorial splendor had often been the subject for his pleasant contemplation. For years the two of them had been shabby leaders of the parish contingent for the procession, but now they both possessed coats that would outwear them both. It was a warm, secure feeling.

Then, with a groan, Dan would roll out of bed, away from his sleeping wife, pull his cricket cap more firmly on his head, for Dan believed that the head deserved a covering just as much as any other part of the sleeping body, straighten his tie, which he wore in bed to keep his throat in good fettle, and stumble across to the window. When he got there he would push it open, draw up a chair, and sit in wait shivering, like a hunter.

Dan would sit like a hunter, and his voice would be his gun. Along the road outside, there would come some gently whirring cyclist on his way to early work. As he passed Dan's window his cycle would often rear like a cow pony before a swaying rattlesnake, for from the window, the until now silently gaping window, there would come a shout like a bullet. It threw normal men from their saddles, and it harmed the feebler ones. Dan always shouted the same thing, for all men in the dark were Joseph to him, so his shout was "Joseph!" and it was a halt sound clear and strong. It never failed.

When the cyclist had picked himself up, and lifted up his vehicle, and had looked around for the projectile voice, Dan would go on in a more normal conversational tone: "What time is it, Joseph?"

There would always be a discernible pause after that. Then from the dismounted rider there would come: "I think it's about five o'clock."

Dan would squirm testily on his seat at that. "Sure I know that. It's about five. If you haven't a watch of your own will you step over to the barber's shop opposite and look at the clock hanging up in the window, there's a good fellow. Here, you can prop your bike up against our railing there."

This rarely led to an altercation, unless it was very wet and stormy. Generally the dismounted one would prop his cycle up, and go across and peer in at the barber's window.

While he was peering Dan was prone to shout at him angrily: "Light a match, man! How in the name of God do you expect to see a clock in the dark?"

After all this, when the time had been given, generally monosyllabically, and the cyclist had driven muttering away, Dan would formally arise. This consisted of taking his tie off and hanging up his cricket cap on a hook behind the bedroom door. Going down, stretching and scratching, wearing his Welsh flannel nightshirt, he would start m-m-meeeing and humming quietly to see if his pipes were in good tune, for Dan was very vain about his voice. He used to sing the Offertory motet nearly every Sunday at the High Mass. He really did have a good powerful baritone voice, but it was not deserving of all the attention that Dan gave it.

By the time that he had got the fire going and the bacon fried on the gas stove, and the tea wetted, Dan would be in great shape. The room would be rocking with the reverberations of his voice. The crockery used to dance on the dresser when he put his head back and gave out with his favorite *Ave Verum*. There was a tremulo piece in it, where he got up to *corpus natum de Maria Virgine,* that was so powerful that the children and Mrs. Furlong used to hear it in their sleep, and it would turn them over smiling.

When the Furlongs first moved in, the neighbors on either side of them shouted and beat their walls until Dan heard them above his own voice, and they begged him to desist. Dan was very contrite about it. He said that in future he would sing sweet and low. After a few days of that the neighbors asked him to go back to full-throated singing, for Dan's low sweet song used to percolate through their walls like a growling, menacing sort of thunder, and their dogs and cats would start scratching and whimpering outside their bedroom doors, pleading to be let in; the terrified animals would gnaw the woodwork in their frenzy, thinking that some new and horrifying sort of electric storm was coming up. Now most of the people around groaned, put the light on, and started reading as soon as the first "Joseph!" toppled over the cyclist.

Dan would sing Palestrina or Gregorian chant as he pulled on his moleskin trousers in front of the kitchen fire. Over his head would go his gray singlet and shirt, and around his neck he would wrap his sweat rag of a scarf. While he was dressing, his mug of tea and his plate of fried bread and bacon would be steaming on the mantelpiece before him. When he had finished his meal, and had a nip of the crayture from the heel of the week-end bottle, he would pull on his reefer jacket and his broken-peaked cap, the uniform of the Cardiff dock-walloper. Through the kitchen, out through the hallway, he would push his cycle, and holding it against him he would roar a rousing to the still sleeping household. It was a muted roar ever since the milkman Connors said his horse dropped dead outside the Furlongs' the first day that he heard it, but there was still a trumpetlike quality to the blast that got the family stirring. Then out into the still dark and muggy morning Dan would wheel his cycle, to join the converging lines of cyclists who were making for the dock gates.

The way that he mounted his cycle was in the manner of all the dockers. They did not regard cycling as a recreation, but as a means of getting to and from the docks. Their cycles often threw them, and cycles generally were considered something

like unfriendly animals. Dan used to prop his cycle up against
the curb, walk away a piece, and then come up on it from behind, somehow crawling on, pushing madly at the curb with the
foot that was not clawing at the pedal. He would go from
side to side of the road in a sort of zigzag until he had gained
the mastery, and then he would straighten up and somehow
jog along, slowly and shakily.

Whenever he came to a corner he would put his hand out,
and would go around it like a plane banking. Every morning
he would draw up to the curb at the home of the Usher Casey,
and the two of them would slowly ride on together. The Usher
was slight and ginger, quiet and gentle, where Dan was loud
and burly, truculent, a joker. They had been raised in adjacent
houses, they had started squirting water on the tipping coal
together, they had become partners as tippers, and they had
graduated in the same year to the job of coal-trimming. They
knew each other so well that they had little to say to each
other as they rode along, but within a few blocks they were
surrounded with cycling dockers, and they would all be
greeting one another. Unless it was summer it would still be
dark and the consequent misdirected hailing could shake the
houses that they were passing worse than did the streetcars.
In sorting out where Johnny was, or who was sick in Timmy
Deasy's house, or where was Larry Ryan, there was a clamor
that was louder and less sweet than a pack of hounds in full
cry.

The dockers, most of the time that they were talking to
themselves, or to one another, had to contend with the clang
of boilermaking, or the crashing of tipping coal, or the welding
of steel plates, so that even in the quiet early morning streets
they contended with the absent noises. If Dan was feeling
chipper or there was plenty of work piling up, he was wont

to break into a hymn as they neared the dockyard gates, so that the whole ruck of dockers would pedal past the gate custodian to the tune of an *Asperges* or maybe a *Magnificat*.

Since last St. Patrick's Day, however, Dan and the Usher had been feeling so contented that they just jogged along on their cycles, leaving the commotion to the others. All the others were very much of the same pattern as the Usher and Dan. The Mauler Sullivan, years ago, had got the contract for the dock labor on the Cardiff docks, and he had made the Welsh quaysides sound like those of Cork and Waterford and Dublin. There was an instance of one Welshman getting a job of the Mauler. He said that his name was Slavin, so the Mauler hired him. When the dockers found out that his real name was Evans they christened him Shamrock, and he worked among them happily for years. The poor fellow, the bold Shamrock, fell down his own chimney one stormy Christmas Eve, attempting to clear an obstruction that was causing it to smoke, and he broke his neck, and that was the end of him.

"Poor old Shamrock," said Dan Furlong when he heard of it — he was working at the time, all coal-begrimed and sweating — "poor old Shamrock. Not content with becoming an Irishman the social climber had to try to be Father Christmas."

They were an Irish society, and they were as conspicuous among the pervading Welshry as are horses amid city traffic, and just as the horses have no desire to turn themselves into motorcars, the Irish had no desire to change themselves either. They were happy as they were. Especially so were the Usher and Dan since they had got their topcoats, for they had both been needing them and had had no hope of getting them until the very eve of St. Patrick's Day.

The previous winter had been a hard one. With the advent of the thirties, fewer and fewer ships were coming in to load up with Welsh steam coal, and the whole area was hit by the depression. Cash buying became a thing of the past, any sort of buying was cut down to a minimum, and such as there was was done on the Kathleen Mavourneen system, the credit system, and indeed God knows that it did look as though it might be for years and it might be forever before all the payments were made. Such credit as the two families possessed was needed for the children's clothing, and then, with no money at all involved, both the Usher and Dan were set up for life with topcoating.

It meant a lot to both of them, since they led the parish men, as their fathers had before them, in the annual St. Patrick's Day procession. Shabby, they felt ashamed, but now, as long as they lived, they knew that they could walk like kings, and so it was that Dan Furlong's spirit was serene when he woke of mornings, and why the two of them were so quiet and so contented at the docks.

In their genteelly tattered despair, as a last throw, they had turned to their relations, and out of this gamblers' chance had come the coats that were to let them lead the procession like a pair of draggled peacocks for the rest of their walking days, the heartbreak of their households and their own delight.

The Usher had gone to his father, a retired old shipwright. He hated begging, but he wondered whether the old man could see his way clear to putting a down payment on a coat for him. God knows he did not like to ask it. His father had pledged his own house to cover the mortgage of Usher's only a year ago, and the few shillings that he had went on the horses every week, or on the Irish Sweep, hoping for a stake that would send Usher's eldest boy, Willie, through university. Still, the Usher had to tell his plight. The old man stirred a little uneasily at Usher's tale. Then he reached a moment of decision. "Jeremiah," he had said. He alone gave the Usher his proper name. "Jeremiah, I have a topcoat upstairs that I haven't worn since you were a wee one, meaning to leave it to you when I passed on. It's an Irish frieze coat. It was the last one Jerry Coghlan made, thirty years ago, before the shakes cut off his tailoring. They don't make coats like that any more, son. I'll bring it down, so that you can march proudly and properly in my old place, as steward in the procession."

The old man heaved himself up out of his armchair, thumped upstairs, and soon returned with the coat. The Usher gasped for air as the camphorated covering hit him, but the old man slit it open and pulled out the coat. It needed an effort on his part to lift it, so heavy was it, and he laid it on the table and stepped back almost reverently for the Usher to look at it.

The Usher gazed at it with respect, then he picked it up and put it on. He buttoned it up, and it buttoned all the way to the neck, in an archaic sort of fashion. It had velvet lapels and collar, and its original black color had become green with age around the shoulders, but it was a great, hard-wearing overcoat. When he rubbed the quality of the sleeve the Usher said, and meant it, "Begod, Dad, they don't make coats like this any more." The old man was satisfied with the reception that Usher had accorded what was to be his legacy. There was only one thing wrong with it, as far as the old man could see, and that was that the coat had been made for him, who was a far bigger man than the Usher. He looked at it critically.

"It's a bit on the big side, son," he said, "but no matter. Don't let any of them tailors get their hands on it for alteration. Sure they'd steal some of that stuff off the coat, and put some shoddy stuff back. They're crooks, all of them, since Jerry Coghlan, may the Lord have mercy on him and on all the souls of the faithful departed. Will you take it with you, son? Or will you leave it here for St. Patrick's Day?"

The Usher could not bear to part with the coat, so he said that he would wear it home, and home he went proudly. There was such a smell of camphor emanating from it that people turned and looked after the Usher as he walked along, but it was little that they could see of him. The coat reached down to his ankles, and the shoulders of the Usher kept slipping through the neck of it, so that it was as if a dark-colored bell were swinging along, with wee Usher as the clapper.

He called on Dan on his way home with it. Dan was sitting in the kitchen, with his music in front of him and his pipes going strong as he m-m-meed a new *Introit* for next Sunday. Mrs. Furlong put her face in her hands when she saw the Usher, and hustled the three younger children out into the scullery, where they all started laughing over something. Dan looked at the coat silently. He sat a full minute silently letting the sight of the Usher in his topcoat sink in. Then he said: "Begod, Usher, you've got a coat there. It's a grand coat, man. You want to work your shoulders a bit to keep the neck of it up, but it's a topcoat the Bishop couldn't buy these days."

Dan sighed, and took his spectacles off. He went on: "You know, Usher, God has been good to us. Here we were yesterday a pair of ragged dockers, and today we both look like a pair of Solomons." He raised his voice. "Jerry, are you studying upstairs? Can you hear me?" By this time the Usher was holding down the cups that were dancing on the table. "Are you up there, Jerry boy?" Dan winked at the Usher. "Bring down my new topcoat, there's a good lad."

Dan turned to the Usher. "You see, Usher, I've not been idle either. I went around to my brother Joe and put it to him fairly and squarely. You know Joe is doing well with his insurance peddling and only five children. I told Joe that since remembered time the elder Furlong and the elder Casey had marched ahead in the St. Patrick's Day procession, and that it was up to him to lend me a coat. Begod, I hadn't put the bite on him since Christmas, and he came through. Wait now, here's Jerry with it, and you'll see it." Dan grinned delightedly as son Jerry brought the coat in, with a schooled straight face. "Begod, Usher, Joe can kiss this coat good-by. It's a lovely coat, man, too good for Joe. Wait now, till you see me in it."

Dan picked up the coat, which almost shimmered in the electric light. It was a herringbone tweed of such a pattern that only an uninhibited movie director would wear it in this country. Joe was a frustrated artist, and this purchase had been his last revolt against his bourgeois wife and life. He was glad when Dan called for it, and he lent it for good, so he hoped. Dan put it on. It was a double-breasted coat, and it would have been tight for the Usher, for Joe was a scrawny wee fellow. Dan had to let out his breath to get into it, and then he could fasten only the bottom button. The sleeves were crawling up his arms like live things. He looked expectantly at the Usher, and his expectations were rewarded.

The Usher, standing there in his greening frieze tent of a topcoat, spoke out his admiration. "Be-dam now, Dan, that's a fine bold coat. It fits snugly, too. There won't be a pair of such dapper stewards from any of the parishes next Sunday." Away went the Usher, glad that Dan had been lucky too. Nora Casey, the Usher's wife, looked at him when he came in proudly, and her eyes filled with tears, but she said, somehow, "Yes, Usher, that's a grand coat." What else could she say, or what could Mary Furlong say? They were grand coats.

Dan and the Usher led the parade upon the following Sunday. It was the turn of their parish, the dockers' parish, to take the vanguard, and boldly they stepped out. They were all festooned with shamrock that had been blessed and distributed after the morning Masses, and their derby hats were atilt, and they swung their stewards' wands like shillelaghs — and they were wearing their coats. Dan's coat was so tight around him that it made him high-step, and any gust of wind blew the Usher's coat against his legs so that he would have lost his footing if the coat had not borne him up. They were a pair of peacocks all right, although their wives wept quietly as they saw them pass, and their children blushed. The worst apprehensions of their families were not realized, for after the procession they both put away their coats in camphorated wrappings for the next year. They were too good for every Sunday wear.

The coats were a sort of turning point for the Usher and for Dan, and for all the dockers. The work began to pick up, their children started to graduate, the Furlongs got an electric clock that Dan suspected but respected, so that cyclists passed his window unscathed in the mornings. Dan and the Usher and their like were so sure of themselves that they raised their families decently, somehow paid off the Johnny Fortnights until Kathleen Mavourneen came to mean a song again, and through all their dirty, hard, and dangerous docker work they walked sure-footed to a happy death. Even if they borrowed sometimes they were always good security.

# XVI

## WHERE FALLS NOT HAIL

CORPORAL EUMENIDES, squatting on his hunkers, was teaching his three companions how to speak the English language. Somehow or other, supplies had got mixed up, and the brigade had received a supply of school readers designed to teach the children English. General Xanthos was a wise man; he had kept the books and issued them to the soldiers, to the two thousand of them. The books were colored picture books of King Arthur and his Knights of the Round Table, and the corporal was reading out loud, in his best Levantine English, which was not very good, the story of Arthur's dying, and of the hand coming up out of the lake to grasp the sword; the recruits were frowning, staring at the pictures in their copies. They were all on different pages, so that when the corporal would break into Greek to explain what he was talking about, they all looked more closely at their books, avoiding one another's eyes, being ashamed of their ignorance, and as yet being strange to one another, the three of them having been newly drafted.

Corporal Eumenides knew that this was so, but he liked the story so much that he went on reading it silently to himself, while his three pupils, squatting like him, silently turned over the pages of the books and looked at the pictures. It was all very peaceful and sunny, pleasant and quiet, nicer than it really was, because they knew that on the next day they were going into the line again. It was getting toward late afternoon on that day, when Corporal Eumenides looked up from his reading and saw coming toward him a man who looked like the Gawain of his picture book, and with him, walking behind, was his squire.

The sun was behind the fair man and his follower as they drew near, and its slanting rays gilded them, and the dust that their walking made was like a mist around their feet. They walked up silently toward Eumenides in the fading day, and he thought that they were like people out of the past, out of the picture book that told of Avalon, where Arthur and the knights that were close to his bosom held eternal holy carouse, save when they came down from their Olympus to help good causes.

They are already a legend in the land, Harold Childe, the fair young Englishman, and his Gurkha servant, Johnny, who came from the hill state of Nepal, which is adjacent to India. This is surprising, for it is but a brief time since the two of them first came walking up the cobbled street of Nicossa toward the monastery where the Sacred Brigade had its headquarters.

Corporal Eumenides watched them coming up, with a curiosity that he did not show; but as they approached, he slowly rose to his feet from where he had been squatting in the shadow cast by an armored car, and awaited them. He stood erect and helmeted like a soldier, while his companions, newly drafted, clumsily got up, too, and doffed their American helmets like peasants, and stood deferentially.

The Englishman and his dark, squat servant had been traveling hard, coming from no one knew where. There was a film of dust over them, and although they were lightly accoutered, and bearing only side arms, they were near to exhaustion — that was plain to see. Harold Childe was panting slightly as he began to speak, slowly and pedantically, in the liquid classical tongue of the country.

"Tell me, soldier, is this the camp of the Sacred Brigade, and if so, where is the General Xanthos with his forces?"

Corporal Eumenides pulled his eyes away from the chased and polished handle of the long knife that Harold Childe was wearing in a scabbard at his side, and he answered in his barbarous hill dialect, while his three companions looked on at him respectfully, "It is, Excellence. If you will but follow me I shall conduct you to his place."

Leaving the three recruits amazed at the ease with which their corporal conversed with the English milord, he led Harold Childe and Johnny to the gates of the monastery. Along the walls there were jeeps and propped-up motorcycles; and two sentries, with Tommy guns under their oxters, straightened up from their slouching when they saw Corporal Eumenides come near with the strange pair that he was escorting. The pair of strangers looked like soldiers; dark patches showed up on their sun-bleached khaki-twill tunics where they had removed their insignia and badges of rank. Harold Childe was wearing the green bonnet of a rifle regiment perched neatly on his head, and Johnny was wearing at a jaunty angle a wide-brimmed hat, the sort that was affected by the Indian and the Australian infantry. Corporal Eumenides stopped importantly in front of the sentinels.

"Here," he said, "is an excellence and his body servant, come to speak with the General Xanthos. I shall leave him in your care."

With that, the stocky little soldier turned toward the tall young Englishman and saluted him formally, and then he grinned, because he saw that Johnny was grinning widely at him from behind Harold Childe. Walking off, he went back to enjoy the aroused respect of the three recruits whom he had previously impressed with his tales of the war against the Italians and the Germans, and about the girls of Alexandria.

There was no doubt in the minds of the sentinels at all as they looked at Harold Childe and his servant. Here were no crazy indoctrinated Bulgars come into the lion's den disguised to kill their leader. Without hesitation, they let their weapons trail and pushed open the massive gates of the monastery, calling out for the sergeant of the guard. At once he conducted them into the cool, tiled quietness of the monastery waiting room, and although it was the time of siesta, General Xanthos was with them in the space of minutes, wide eyed and interested, buttoning up his tunic and still holding in his hand, that was as thick and as pudgy as a badger's paw, the book of children's readings about Arthur and his knights that he had been leafing through while waiting for sleep to come to him. The general was a big, dark, burly man. The pompadour of his hair was thick and graying, and his heavy mustache curved up, flaring beyond his weathered and creased cheeks like the horns of a ram. He was a good Greek.

Harold Childe, unsmiling, grave, with the intimidating courtesy of the gently born, faced the general and unbonneted as he spoke.

"General," he said. "I am Harold Childe. Once I commanded a company of riflemen that fought on the flank of your brigade at El Alamein. I have come here with my servant Johnny, who was my military runner, to offer my services to you." He was speaking in an archaic form of Greek, classical and stilted. He went on, "The English have been left too poor after their strife, and they are too preoccupied with their own dire needs to help you as they would wish. So I have come, with my servant, as a token."

While he was speaking the declining sun was beaming behind him through a west window, and it made him somehow
shining, and that, along with his antique mode of speech, gave
him an appearance of remoteness, so that General Xanthos
blinked somewhat as Harold Childe went on, fingering the
pommel of his side arm, "There will be no international com-
plications if you use us and we are taken. There is no record of
us in army rolls, and we will leave you when our task is done,
so that you will not have to explain us. I am a soldier of some
experience, having served in many lands. I will help you in
your fight."

General Xanthos did not hesitate. Although there was something here that he did not understand, he was glad of this
man's proffering. The English always had a kind of respect for
the Greeks, even if the present swarthy ones did not jibe with
the slim and fair young classics that the English read about in
their schools. There had been Byrons; it seemed as if there
still were. He started talking in the rather staccato-accented
English that he had learned in Egypt, where he had lived after
escaping from Crete with the New Zealanders.

"You are welcome, sir, you and your servant. Since you must
bear a name with us, I shall call you Byronides." He said that
with an engaging scoundrelly sort of soldier's grin. "As for
Johnny, he shall remain Johnny. Now come, Byronides, and
meet my staff. We drink tea at this hour, being now on British
rations. I shall give you a company in one of my battalions.
They are going forward tomorrow night." He took his rein-
forcement by the arm, but Harold Childe — or Byronides, as
he was to be known — resisted gently, pulling his arm free,
and said, "It would be better" — and he spoke in English now,
in a high-pitched Etonian sort of English, and so more quickly
— "if you would let me form a battle patrol, sir. That is what

I am most adept at using. I don't think that your opposites have anything really like it."

A smile grew and deepened the creases on the face of General Xanthos as he heard the importunity of this fair stranger. "Fine," he said. "That is what it will be. It solves all sorts of problems. We are not good at patrols — we talk too much — but you and your Gurkha — I remember the likes of you coming slinking back through our lines in Africa. That's it, then. I'll have it announced on orders tonight, and you will have all the volunteers that you can use, come the morning. Come now," he said, grinning, "Byronides; we shall drink some tea."

Johnny had vanished from the door of the waiting room where he had been standing, long before this time. That old soldier had sought out the cook house, and grinning and silent, was sipping down a mug of hot sweet tea, wherein the canned milk was curlingly dissolving, while the cooks and their help stood around him grinning back at him, and saying, *"Tik hai, Johnny,"* which is the greeting for Gurkha soldiers the world over.

In the brigade mess, General Xanthos hid his smiling as he watched the new recruit begin to operate. He barely touched hands with the other combat officers, but devoted himself to the thick-fingered, dour, and suspicious commissary officer. That showed how real an old campaigner was this Byronides. All at once the general felt as hopeful as if trucks of supplies had come to him; Byronides was more welcome to him than good news.

After the tea drinking, which the Greeks politely forced down, hoping for coffee soon, the old sweat of a commissary officer gave Byronides a room of his own above a garage, on the other side of the town square from the monastery. He got the garage cleared and cleaned out for him. Before night fell, the grim old Greek giver had issued Byronides infantry stores for forty men and all the specialist weapons of an infantry company. Then, with an effort that was worthy of a descendent of Hercules, he issued a jeep from his precious transport pool to the newly arrived one, and, exhausted with his giving, turned over a light truck also for the transport of the to-be-formed patrol. It was his way of showing what he thought of Byronides, for, being a simple man, nearly illiterate, he had more of a feeling for what Byronides was than more worldly ones.

The next morning after the first parade, men began to assemble in the square before the garage, waiting for Byronides to appear, so that they could volunteer for his patrol. The story of his coming had already spread through the village camp, and, as soldiers will, they had embroidered and decorated the story with their telling, so that, despite their shy, passive waiting, all the soldiers were excited inside, anxious to see the milord. All of them had heard stories of the English lords, and they had all seen pictures of the jousting knights of Arthur in their new books. They did not say much to one another while they waited. After they had all been there a little while, and it was apparent that no more were coming, Byronides came out of his quarters, clean and shaven, with his khaki pressed, and with his bonnet of rifle green perched squarely on his head, with the strangely carved pommel of his knife standing out gleaming from the scabbard at his side. A little behind him stepped Johnny. The soldiers looked at them intently, yet shyly, and after a little while, after Byronides had looked at them, he began to speak.

"Oh, men," he said to them in his liquid classical Greek, "we have come here to teach you a way of making war. It is a hard and bloody way. Some of you will die learning, and most of us will have passed away ere this year passes; for when the

way is learned it must be practiced, and —" he smiled — "the
enemy will resent our lore, and they will seek to encompass
our destruction. Now, there are too many soldiers here, so
first let all the married ones who have children step forward,
and then let the married ones also. . . . Now that there are
far too many still in the ranks, let those step backward who
have fought in Africa."

There were nearly a score of single veterans from the war in
Africa, and to them Johnny and his captain added ten men
more. The rest were sent back to their units, and then, without
a word to his selected men, Byronides stepped back and motioned Johnny forward.

The little Gurkha suddenly became a sergeant stiff and
straight. He stood in front of his new squad, and in Urdu,
which is the lingua-franca of the armies of India, and which
these men did not in any way understand, he called them to
attention, and the urgency in his voice brought them up stiff
and straight. Then he dressed them in ranks of three, and led
them at a jog trot to the edge of town, where Byronides was
waiting for them in his jeep, with his leg thrown negligently
over the side as if it were a charger.

The training started that very morning. Out there in the
dusty olive groves those heavy-handed, plodding peasants were
taught to crawl and to walk without making a sound. Byronides
and Johnny walked like ghosts among them, coming up silently
from behind them, and showing how they could have killed
their recruits silently. There was something uncanny in the way
that Byronides and Johnny prowled, so that their men would
cross themselves backward, in the Greek fashion, after they
had passed by them, and breathe deeply.

For weeks they did nothing but learn to walk silently, and
their hands — their calloused hands that used to swing from

their sides — became supple, writhing, strangling hands, for nightly, after their days outdoors, in the garage, which had become their headquarters, Johnny used to teach them to kill by using the hands and arms alone. Byronides was never there at night, for as soon as the daily training was completed, he used to mount his jeep and ride up to the brigade line, and he reconnoitered every yard of it all through the enemy's wire and his mines.

After weeks of unarmed training, all the patrol were supplied with machetes, which are used for cutting undergrowth. These, under Johnny's direction, they honed and ground until they became sharp killing knives. Then he brought out his kukri, which is the curve-bladed weapon of the Gurkhas, and Byronides pulled out his shining knife from its greased scabbard, and the men learned how to slice and slash until their weapons became extended arms.

After a month of training, one sunny early morning at their first parade, Byronides came out and looked at them, and smiled and went away. The men had changed. There was a spring in their bearing, they stood proudly, their machetes hung by their sides as if they belonged there — they hung snugly. Then Johnny stepped in front of them, grinning, and dismissed them. They knew that their time of action had come.

That night, after a meal served an hour earlier, and while it was still light, the patrol piled into their light truck and headed for the front. They had smeared their faces with black soot, and had festooned themselves with drab coverings, and had hidden the shining thirst of their knives under a greasy layer. The few carabineers had weapons so tended that they came apart like well-cooked chicken meat. They looked like killers, and the tall, fair young leader looked more deadly than the rest.

Just as dusk was falling they dismounted behind the line and waited for the blanket of the dark to cover them. They melted into the landscape, and lay there silently for hours, until Byronides clicked his tongue, and they fell in behind him. They moved up and passed through the lines, crouched and silent, on their way to killing. The infantrymen looked up at them out of their dank and smelling holes, and wished them well, hoping at the same time, like all infantrymen, that these fly-by-nights would not bring too much grief down upon their bowed heads, who would still be holding there, when the special men had returned to Nicossa and were sleeping easy.

Dawn was coming up as Byronides led his patrol back. The morning ground mist was swirling around them as they trotted back through the company lines, and the infantrymen saw that they were all sticky with blood, more like butchers than like soldiers. Byronides was carrying his knife tucked underneath his arm, and the rest of the patrol were carrying their machetes out away from them. In the midst of the patrol, as silent as their captors, were three prisoners. One of them was dressed in the uniform of a neighboring state, and the two others were dressed in the uniforms of guerrillas — quiet, clerklymen, obviously headquarters personnel, cipher clerks, and secretaries. The three of them had the stiff, strained look of men who had seen the reeking, spouting, grating shambles that accompanies an attack with knives. They were all witless from fear, and they shivered as they trotted stumblingly, not from cold, but from memory.

That was the start of their action. Night after night Byronides led them over, until the whole of the brigade front was aflame. They slept by day, and many of them died, but always there were more Greeks to step in. Corporal Eumenides had become the chief one among the Greeks. He and Johnny were the council of Byronides. He, a peasant Greek from the hills, watched the two strangers closely, and wondered about them.

The tide was turning in their favor. The guerrillas were giving ground. Within weeks the end would be, and there was jubilation at the green tables, and a faint feeling of hope even entered into the hearts of the infantrymen.

One day General Xanthos came to call on the patrol in their headquarters. He waved them all down as they stood up for him, and climbed up the ladder to the room of Byronides, where that one was squatting on his bed, cleaning and honing his long knife. It was a weapon of exquisite workmanship, such as the general had not seen before. When Byronides looked up and saw the general, he thrust the knife into its scabbard carefully, and smiled and stood up.

"Byronides," said the general, motioning him to sit as he heavily sat himself down on a packing case, "things are good. One more thrust and the guerrillas will have lost the hills, and then it will be over, and you and Johnny will be on your way." He looked quizzically at Byronides. "What is your way, son?"

Byronides looked at him gravely, unsmiling, silent; yet it was peaceful in that upper room.

The general said, "I never expected you to answer that, nor did I wish to know. It was just to show you that I think I know how and whence you came, and if I did not believe that, I would not care to live on. Now, as to next week, next Thursday at midnight, when our push begins —" They went into plans and maps until all was clear.

From that time on, the patrol just rested, waiting for Thursday. They did not train; they slumped into an easy way, relishing all the time of it. Then, on that Thursday before dusk fell, they moved up to the line, all loaded down with infantry paraphernalia, for they were going in to spearhead this last foray, and they needed ammunition, flares, mortars, food, and water.

At midnight they went over the top, and within an hour Byronides flared back the news that they had overrun the forward defenses of the enemy. The general advance went in, and there was bloody, roaring, smoky fighting. The patrol broke up unofficially, and each man went his way. Corporal Eumenides, about 3 a.m., saw Johnny and Byronides running lightly ahead of him, the knives hanging loose from their wrists. There was a whistle and a crash and a flash where they had been. It was on a side of a lake, and when Eumenides got there the two of them were lying on the ground, sorely wounded and near to death.

There was a deep dark stain around the grass where Byronides lay crumpled, and Johnny was on his knees, his feet a bloody pulp. The noise of battle was going from that spot beside the lake, and victory seemed to be assured. Corporal Eumenides ran back, stumbling and panting, bloodied and exhausted. A jeep pulled up in front of him, and the corporal saw that the only occupants were General Xanthos and his driver. With no ceremony, Eumenides piled in.

"They are hit, Excellence. Johnny and he both, up by that lake yonder!" He pointed.

General Xanthos turned the jeep toward the lake; heedless of mines, he raced to the spot where the two had been lying, but when they arrived there was no sign of them. There was no sign of them at all, only the bloodstained ground, and the noise of battle going from that place. Where Byronides had been, there was his bloody knife. The general and the corporal looked at each other. It was eerie at that place in the dim light that comes before sunup. The birds had started faintly twittering. General Xanthos picked up the knife and swung it up and down in his hand, looking at Eumenides, whose thoughts were going along with his own. Then he stepped back, and he flung the knife as hard as he could over the lake. It soared through the air, and the first rays of the sun gilded it before it fell into the water, which seemed to receive it. Suddenly the birds were in full song, and as General Xanthos and Corporal Eumenides remounted the jeep and drove back to Nicossa, to await the return of their victorious brigade, the sun came up over Greece.

# XVII

## SOLITARY DOGAN

THE others were killed or got out of it, but Dogan stayed right on to the end. Always fresh and smiling, he was deader than the killed ones. He lived in the strange half-world which creatures inhabit, and when Bluey Northcott first saw him that day, years after the war, in the smoky bedroom of the Hotel Normandie, he was the same solitary, unchanging Dogan who still drank too deeply, who still went to church, who flew unscathed while all around him his fellows flamed to death.

Vincent Dogan came into the hotel bedroom where Bluey and the others were trying to play poker after drinking too much. He stood in the doorway, years younger than they, clean and fresh in a light tweed suit. He said "Good evening" in a way that showed that he had been to a good English school — Ampleforth or Downside most likely — but the way that he said it showed that he was no Englishman. He had an Irishman's look about him, and the faintest touch of a brogue in his speech. "Good evening," he said again, smiling at them.

Bluey and the rest of them looked at him. "Who the hell are you?" said Sam. Sam had come out from Seattle, and had begun to wish that he hadn't. "Who the hell are you?"

"I'm Vincent Dogan," said he, "and I've come to command you."

At that the two young limeys, all suède shoes and accent, stared at him.

"B-but," said Holroyd, with his hardly affected stammer, "w-we'd already decided that Northcott here was to lead us."

Dogan still stood there smiling. Bluey knew from that moment that Dogan was to command.

The other limey, with fair flaring mustaches, began to look less dopey. "Are you the Vincent Dogan that commanded the Polish group from Haslemere?"

Dogan nodded at that, and Sam relaxed, because it was evident from the way the two limeys and Bluey Northcott reacted that it was going to be all fine, but Dogan kept staring at Bluey.

"Hello, Northcott; don't you remember me? I was over your mess a few times in England, with Leo Kenny; he came from Sydney. You're from Melbourne, aren't you? Can I have a drink now?"

Bluey poured Dogan a half tumbler of Carmel hock, and Dogan sat on the edge of the bed and swallowed it quickly, the way he always drank.

The others stopped trying to play poker, and just tried to study Dogan. They knew, all of them, that in encountering him the time was beginning to run out for some of them. Dogan had become a legend before the late great was even half over. He had become a fighter ace even before Pearl Harbor, and by the time Uncle Sam had started sweeping over the English Channel, young Dogan, in his early twenties, was making command decisions, and still flying. Now all these once-fliers had met together, flying fighters in a two-bit war, and getting a check deposited in a home bank for every month of it. None of them really knew what they were aiding by their combat. It might have been the Commies, although they hoped it wasn't. Anyhow, what the hell? They had got their wings again, they were all fit for flying, not for much else.

After V-J Day, Bluey Northcott had gone back clerking for the Bank of Australia; Sam had tried it out at Boeing's; the limeys were hoping to clean up enough on this show to let them start something outdoors and gentlemanly. Holroyd, the Yorkshireman, was probably going to join up with Bluey in a bush-flying venture in Western Australia, and Eaton was hoping to get started on a fruit farm in the Canadian Okanagan Valley. They were all out here for something somewhere else, except Dogan. Bluey, they knew, would have put on a respectable show with the squadron, enough to convince the wogs who were paying them, but Bluey wouldn't have taken any chances, there would have been no Battle of Britain stuff about their weaving. Now, just as if somebody had left a window open, they all grew a little chill and gray as they looked at the smiling, solitary Dogan.

In the morning, Bluey and the others met Dogan in the lounge, just as they were going down to breakfast. Still smiling — he was always smiling — he was asking the hall porter where the nearest church was. With a start, Bluey remembered it was Sunday, so he went to Mass with Dogan, while the others passed in to breakfast. Just as they were finishing, Bluey and Dogan came back, and the others sat and smoked and waited for them.

Holroyd had been interned here for a while during the war, while Pétain still Vichey-ed it, so after breakfast they strolled around the Place du Canon, like football stars strolling on the campus, and tried to ignore the delighted smiles of the people, who nudged one another as they passed, and who rolled their eyes and shook their heads delightedly when they thought of the fate of the guerrillas, once these fliers started blasting them.

All Sunday was quiet and peaceful; it was the last of those days for most of them. On Monday morning, Mr. Londros, the Americanized agent who had bought them, came into the hotel after them, bowing and smiling. None of them liked him. He smiled too much, patted too much on the back, and he was a blooming civilian. Still, he was depositing those monthly checks in the banks back home, the checks that were to save them from those lives of menial mediocrity, of quiet constant anxiety, that the Air Forces had taken from them. He had come to take them out to the airport, to their weapons and their planes. They bundled into his waiting car, and in ten minutes they were walking around the seven Spitfires that Londros had got hold of somehow.

Spitfires Mark IV, they were, but where had been the British rondels there were now the garish designs of a shabby state. It wasn't the rondels that the fliers were concerned about. No longer were they bored, potential material for trouble, but honest craftsmen poring over their tools. They climbed into the planes, they revved them, they crawled all over them. They pulled on their flying clothes with the abstracted air of flying men who do not know how romantic are their appurtenances.

Dogan stood a little apart from them all, with the same smile on his lips. Somehow they all looked at him. He grinned and stuck his thumb up. They all climbed into their planes, staggered, waltzed around, steadied, and roared off. Dogan watched them all take off and then climbed into his plane and joined them. They all naturally fell into formation, and within the first five minutes, for all their mercenary caution, they fell under Dogan, and began to fly for the love of it. When they landed, it was Sam who said to Dogan, "Man! Oh, you man!" He spoke for all of them when he said it. The hell with it. If they were going to fly anyway. . . . This mood lasted all the way back to the hotel.

They left Dogan at the airport. They were all feeling rather played out, except for him. He went into a huddle with the ground crews, and the guy from the Bronx and the little Scots fitter who were handling that end of it knew where they stood when Dogan had finished handling them, with his smile and his brogue. Dogan went back to the hotel about an hour later, happy about the maintenance.

For a week they practiced flying out of the airport. Over the Cedar Mountains they cast their shadows on the snow-clad shoulders, the ruined cities of an earlier civilization heard the roar of their engines as they buzzed those eerie places. The ancient city of Antiphon looked up at them gleaming overhead, and the twin cities of Bala and Gazel saw the flash of their wings. By the end of that week they had become a combat wing, a co-ordinated team.

On the next Monday they moved out to quarters at the airport. Bluey had begun to think that he was getting to know Vincent Dogan by this time. Before this, the young Irishman had been just a tall tale to him. Dogan had been talked about in fighter messes from Scapa Flow to Wanganui. A group captain at twenty-two, the flying Irishman had become an epitome of the few, those happy few, that band of brothers who had kept their gaity in the early days until they died. The only flaw in the legend was that Dogan had not died, but had gone on, smiling, tour after tour, bailing out, collecting gongs, flying, flying, flying, killing, killing, killing.

Dogan began to grow on Bluey. It was amazing how naïve and undeveloped was this fighting man. He had stopped growing properly when he had left school at eighteen to go straight into the Air Force. Dogan loved poetry, but all that he could handle was stuff like the Lake Isle of Innisfree, and Rupert Brooke. He even wrote poetry, which was so bad that it made Bluey shudder, and yet Dogan was very proud of it. The vacant lad had no idea of what was going on in the world. He was like one of those babies or simple people who die in unchristened innocence and walk smilingly through Limbo.

All the rest of them were out in this grubby country for a material reason, and there were others like them in other trouble spots for the same sort of reasons. It all added up, really, to the fact that they were ill-equipped for life and shrank from the drab ways of the disordered peace.

But for no reason like that was the solitary Dogan in the midst of them. He was here because he could be a fighter pilot here; that lonely impulse of fighting flying had ravished him in the way that the love of women has ruined other men. Dogan was too remote ever to have known the earthiness and the delicacy of women. The smiling, gentlemanly Vincent Dogan was just a combat killer flyer. That indeed was all he was.

Gradually, almost imperceptibly, their practice flights began to take them over enemy territory. They shot up a few trucks, cannonaded some slight guerrilla resistance that was holding up the long and ceremonious preparations of the local levies, and got some desultory gunfire directed at them in return. It was on the following Friday, St. William's Day, as Dogan was careful to note in his schoolboy diary, that action really began.

It was on that day that the guerrillas tried to sneak two shiploads of reinforcements across the narrow channel that separated their mountain stronghold from their friendly base

of the adjacent "neutral" country. The guerrillas tried to do
it with fighter cover that was so flagrantly borrowed that the
insigne of the neutral state that had lent the planes was only
perfunctorily smeared over. Dogan and Eaton and Holroyd
met them just as the convoyed tubs were wallowing about
halfway across the narrow channel. They engaged the five
escorting fighters while Bluey and Sam began to cannonade
the ships. Their part was easy. The two old freighters rolled
helplessly, while Bluey and Sam began to rip the ships to
pieces. Futile antiaircraft fire seemed to veer away from them
as if even the tracers were frightened of them, while overhead,
Dogan and the two limeys kept the fighter screen busy. This
screen was Spitfire too.

These neutral Spits were manned by brave, wily, resourceful
fighters, about as native to their country as Dogan and his
company were to theirs. Maybe some of them were planning on
a fruit farm in the Okanagan, or on a bush line in Australia.
As Bluey and Sam flew up from their dismembering to help
Dogan disengage, Eaton's plane blew up, and Holroyd high-
tailed it, with smoke streaming out of his ship. He made it back
to base, but for a while Dogan was all alone up there, while
Bluey and Sam were making height. He sent one enemy plane
shrieking seaward as he turned and twisted to avoid the four
others. Yet even in his desperation he flew in such a way that
one of his pursuers flapped right into Bluey's sights, and so
got as neatly cut in two as if he had passed through a buzz
saw. They all had had enough of it by this time, their gas was
running low, so Dogan and his companions disengaged with
only token resistance from the fighter screen, who were
redundant by this time, as antlike figures kept leaping from
the two killed boats in the channel.

When they swung into the airport they found Holroyd shakily jaunty and eager for a drink. That night Dogan wrote in his slow schoolboy hand to Eaton's mother.

That was the start of their action. From then onward they worked for their money. Dogan led them all the time, every time, and all this while he was training four young Poles who had come to the wing, all grinning and Slavic, as replacements. One of them wouldn't learn. All the time he kept breaking formation and attempting derring-do. He had flown Stormovics and couldn't forget it. At last Dogan shrugged his shoulders, still smiling, and sent him off alone in a quavering, battered old Spit to strafe the Hablum-Gleda road at dusk. He never came back. Dogan knew that he wouldn't. He would never have tried to do that one on his own, even in an airworthy plane. After that, the other Poles caught on and began to fit into the pattern. If they hadn't, Dogan would have killed them too.

Six weeks' hard fighting had nearly worn out the planes. Londros had some new ones lined up at a vague sort of airport in a neutral sort of country, so Dogan, Holroyd, Sam, and Bluey went over to get them. At dawn they were out fussing over the four fairly new War Assets Spitfires, and in the afternoons and evenings they swam, and drank, and lounged, and drank at the local Turf Club. The whole feverish bogus atmosphere suited Dogan absolutely. Waiters in long white robes and cummerbunds pretended that they remembered him when he was flying for the Desert Air Force. Their fawning lying would never have fooled a rookie twice, but Dogan tipped them high for all week. He took eight days of fancy living like a highball, and by the time the planes were ready to fly back, Bluey estimated that Dogan had spent nearly all the money he had made.

They flew out over the blue sea, landed to refuel somewhere

they had been expected, hedgehopped into guerrilla country, shot up a lounging barracks, and got back with only three bullet holes in the whole four fuselages.

Londros was as smooth as a land agent when they got back. He had four more recruits waiting. Two of them were competent Canadians, one was a more than competent German, and the last was a China boy who had done his flying against the Japs. At last the wing had enough planes and enough fliers for shift work.

Every day they were at it, cannonading and machine-gunning. They occasionally acted as artillery for the ground forces, but Dogan so hated serving the grubby generals that there was little of that. Whenever possible they avoided action in the sky. Spitfires were hard to replace, and even harder to refit. Sometimes action was unavoidable, and so Sam was grilled and burnt black to death inside a jammed cowling, and one of the Canadians went down in slowly falling lumps over the guerrilla headquarters of Darsalia. The quiet China boy buzzed too close to earth, and old man Newton reached up and grabbed him.

Dogan had tangled more than any of them. He had shot down at least seven planes, had killed a lot of convoy drivers as he flamed their trucks, and he had almost paused shuddering with his cannons over many troop concentrations. Before the contracted six months were up, Dogan was as deadly as he had ever been.

There were only a few weeks to go, and Bluey and Holroyd were already greedily feeling that six thousand dollars that was almost waiting for them. They had become the old-timers of the wing, and the gradual flow of recruits always listened to them respectfully. Dogan was as remote and as smiling as ever. Bluey had given up any idea of knowing him, months past. The two of them knew that he would remember them, the way he remembered all the men he had flown with, living or dead. He never forgot any of them. He kept up a terrifically detailed and inane correspondence with men and widows and mothers all over the globe. He was godfather to dozens of babies. For all that he wrote, he might just as well have been a dead man writing. He could no more understand the peaceful thrust and pattern of their lives than he could have fought on foot when there was a chance to fly.

The last action left Bluey and Holroyd shaken. Maybe it was because it was the last action. Maybe it was that, but the enemy fighters seemed to know it and really crowded them. They were lucky to get out of it, and they would have been buried in some foreign field for sure if it had not been for Dogan, who maneuvered a newcomer into place as fall guy in order to save his two quaking veterans. The newcomer was shot down instead of them. Dogan knew they were through. Their bank balances were worrying them; the adventure was wearing thin for them.

That night, in the bedroom of the Hotel Normandie, they were having a farewell party, the three of them that were left. They were drinking too much. As usual, Dogan was sucking down every drink as if it were his last. Londros came in to say good-by. If they felt like coming back — smiling at Holroyd and Bluey — why, just let him know. Or maybe they might know some friends? Captain Dogan was staying, of course. Captain Dogan was staying.

Bluey turned and looked at him, and Dogan smiled and said, "Yes, Bluey, I'm staying."

Londros left, and the three of them went on with their drinking, but none of them knew why.

Next morning, as Holroyd and Bluey came down to breakfast, they saw Vincent Dogan coming back from Mass. All the days of his life Dogan would love the bells and the chasubles, the Hail Marys and the candles that were religion to him. The knowledge of the Son of God was as much beyond him as was the Trinity beyond the comprehension of a dog. Bluey at last felt the right feeling for smiling, solitary Dogan. He felt sorry for him. He saw the rest of Dogan's life so clearly that he winced. Dogan would go on flying, getting bilked and cheated by Londros and turbaned waiters for as long as they wanted him. He would drink more and more as his assignments got fewer and fewer. He would fly until he got so shaky that nobody would let him take any sort of plane up.

Nobody would ever shoot Dogan down, nor would he ever crash a plane. Bluey saw that Dogan's hell would go on for years, and he not knowing it until it would frenzy him. Slowly the trim clean figure would rot and bloat. All his face would become bulbous and lined, and he would talk with a whisky wheeze. Then, when humiliation had broken him, Dogan would go down to that Limbo where are the souls of all the unaware people since the world began, and nobody would remember how lovely and sad and deadly and shining had been Vincent Dogan in the days of his youth.

# XVIII

## THE PIPER PAYS

They were both Americans, the Canadian kept insisting, both Americans, and by dint of the amount of wine that the pair of them had drunk the argument kept them happy. It was not very good wine, a thick, heavy, sweet local vintage called Lachryma Christi, but, barring the ordinary wine, it was the best that Sorrento had to offer in the summer of 1944.

The streets of the little Italian bay town were full of British, Canadian, American, and New Zealand junior officers in those days, for convalescent homes had been established there for them, so that they could get a sick leave before rejoining their units after hospital discharge.

There was a certain amount of fraternization among the officers, although not very much, so that, while it was not odd to see the Canadian officer drinking and dining with the American officer, it was not very common either. There were not many tables in the little hillside restaurant, the proprietor had asked them whether they would mind sharing a table, and they did not, and that was how they had become acquainted.

The food was better in other restaurants, notably in the Albergo Tramontano and in the Albergo Lorelei, but both those places were in the town itself, whereas this little place was about three miles out of town, on the way to Amalfi, and it was perched on the side of the cliff, so that from the balcony, where the dinners were served alfresco, the Bay of Naples lay

below, crawling and heaving and glinting, while across the
water twinkled in the sea the reflected lights of the Naples
water front. At that time it needed an actual air raid to douse
the pier lights of Naples, for the invasion of the south of France
was being mounted there, and there was toiling all through the
night.

The little restaurant was not so spoiled by the advent of the
liberators as were the more convenient restaurants. Among the
clientele dining there were quite a few Italians, down from
Rome; and, very much at home there, were the sergeants of a
Quartermaster Corps unit that was stationed adjacent, who
had made it into a sort of mess for themselves. The Canadian
and the American had found it independently on a previous
occasion, and dining alone, they had felt rather out of things,
so they were glad of each other's company.

They had introduced themselves to each other. Angus
Cameron was the Canadian, a tall red-haired captain of the
Manitoba Rifles, and the American was Harland Davis, a
lieutenant in the 88th Infantry Division. In their undress
uniforms — they were both wearing only shirts and slacks,
no badges of rank or insignia showing — they bore a close
resemblance to each other; it was obvious that they were infantry officers, and although Davis was of a saturnine cast, and
was heavier, common experiences during the past few months,
from the Garigliano crossing up to the Gothic Line, had im-
parted a look of kin to them.

Both of them had taken their time arriving. At the hotel
bars, about five o'clock every evening, a few bottles of gin
and whisky were available on the basis of first come, first
served, and they had taken advantage of that at their respec-
tive hotels. Then — well, it was an uphill three miles to the
little restaurant, so there had been pauses a few times on the

way up, at shabby little drinking places, so that both of them
had drink taken before the meal began. By the time it was
over, they had killed three bottles of Lachryma Christi, and
they were arguing, quietly and pleasantly, about which of
them was the real American, or whether they both were, or
whether Canadians were British.

It was pleasant in the little restaurant, nice and gentle.
Everybody was talking quietly; some were smiling slightly at
the sound of one of the American Quartermaster Corps sergeants trying to tell the proprietor something, within the house,
in a mixture of Neapolitan and Brooklynese. Angus Cameron
got the idea that it might be a good idea to switch from the
wine, and, instead of having another bottle, to take on some
liqueur — some anisette or some cognac. He was looking
around for the proprietor or for the proprietor's brother, a
rather exotic-looking Italian who spoke English fairly well, and
who wore riding boots and a flying helmet when he rode his
bicycle, claiming to be the flying column of a partisan group,
but neither of them was around. The brother was probably
within, in the kitchen, helping his brother to understand the
sergeant, but over on the side of the balcony, beyond the
Italian diners, Angus saw a group of French officers. The
French, since their great feat of arms around Cassino, had
held themselves proudly, but aloofly. Angus had never spoken
to one of them, but, because he liked the French and because
he was high with wine, he got to his feet and motioned Harland
to follow him.

Angus stopped at the table of the French officers and looked
down at them. Somehow it seemed that all the Frenchmen became aware of him at the same time, for an almost immediate
hush fell on the table, and they all looked up at him, question-
ing, proud, unsmiling, and, for all their American attire, all

seeming very French. Angus had stopped at the head of the table, and there was seated, in his proper place, a grizzled brigadier, with the medals of Indo-China and of Africa indicated by ribbons, besides the medals of the 1914–1918 combat. The brigadier, after a first glance, had dropped his eyes, so that Angus was looking down at a tough old soldier who showed only by his silence that he was waiting for some explanation of this intrusion.

Angus cleared his throat and said, with a French accent that was not bad at all, for a Winnipegger, "Permit me to congratulate you on the liberation of Paris."

Even while he was talking, the general looked up at him. Paris had been freed but a few days. Paris, that he and his company loved in a way that no German ever loved Berlin; Paris, the heart of the world. Nothing could stop Angus when he saw that his words were doing good. He remembered one of Josephine Baker's songs, and went on, in his Canadian-schoolboy accent: "I have two loves — my country, and Paris." By this time the French were on their feet, and the brigadier was smiling and proffering his hand, really moved, but Angus politely declined, took a deep breath, and, remembering something of Charles Morgan, he went on, "Your Paris is not a city; it is an idea necessary to our civilization."

He knew when to stop; he had shot his bolt, and it had gone straight to the heart of the French. They were all standing up, their napkins in their left hands where their sword pommels used to be, and with their right hands they were offering Angus and his bemused companion, Harland, their friendship. Harland knew that he was in on something. He had noticed how the French kept themselves to themselves, so that he was as pleased as Angus at being asked to join them.

Somewhere or other the French had got hold of some magnifi-

cent lobsters, and the table was covered by the littered remains
of them. The brigadier saw Angus and Harland looking at the
relics, and he called down the table, sharply, but like papa,
"Bambino!" At that, a little Frenchman, a cadet officer —
what the French call an *aspirant* — hurried up to the head of
the table, and the brigadier instructed him in hurried, muttered
French, while two of the captains, one on each side of the
brigadier, pressed Angus and Harland into their seats and
moved down the table.

The brigadier sat down and from underneath the table,
from a bucket with ice in it, brought up a chilled bottle of
good Algerian wine that the French must have brought with
them, and poured a glass of it for Angus, another for Harland,
another for himself, then clinked the glasses together, and
toasted them, smiling, and in a few minutes everything was
friendly and easy. The proprietor came out, scraping, followed by the *aspirant,* and in front of Harland and in front of
Angus he set two magnificent lobsters that the French must
have brought along extra to pay for the cost of the service.

Breaking the lobsters up and eating, drinking the good
wine, talking with gestures and with very tenuous French, for
none of the French officers seemed to have any English, Angus
and Harland felt that the evening was becoming a great
success. They had broken the ice, for even the Italians now
looked across at the table of them and nodded, and raised their
glasses and smiled, gesturing toward Naples, where the invasion
fleet was mounting, showing that they knew that the French
would soon be going into France, and wishing them well.

After about a half hour of this, one of the American Quartermaster sergeants came up and tapped Angus on the shoulder
very politely.

"Excuse me, sir," he said, "but would you gentlemen mind

if we moved your table over to the side of the balcony?"
Angus looked up at him beamingly, and the sergeant went on,
so respectfully, "You see, sir, we are holding a sort of a dance
here tonight, and with your table here — well, it's on the dance
floor. Do you mind, sir?"

"Not at all, sergeant, not at all," said Angus, pleased at being
an interpreter. He explained the position to the brigadier, who,
with smiles and shrugs, joined Angus, only in dumb show, in
letting the sergeant know that everything was fine.

Three or four sergeants and some Italians moved the table
and chairs over for them, and they sat down again, right up
against the balcony. By that time all the rest of the tables had
been cleared away, and an Italian band, in which the big cello
was the major instrument, began to tune up, and some local
Italian peasant girls, with whom the Quartermaster sergeants
had obviously reached some kind of agreement, began to drift
onto the balcony, giggling, in twos and threes. It was a lovely
starlit evening; the scene had a bucolic pleasantness about it,
and the French officers and their two guests pulled their chairs
around so that they could watch the scene.

The band started to play. The sergeants and their girls
shuffled around on the tiled floor, some of them quite gracefully.
It seemed like a nice party, and the French watched it, smiling
and interested.

The brigadier, on an impulse in an interval between the
dances, called up the *aspirant,* whom all of them called
Bambino, and another young man, a second lieutenant. He
spoke to them rapidly, beyond the comprehension of Angus or
of Harland, and he pushed them, while they smilingly pro-
tested, with his hand toward the dance floor. Angus saw then
that he was trying to do his bit for the occasion by asking his
young men to circle the floor once or twice with two of the local
girls, just to show.

The Bambino and his friend went up, bowed formally, and requested two of the girls to dance with them just as the music started. The girls were obviously very flustered at being asked to dance with French officers, for they knew that their partners would never normally have asked them, war or no war, were it not for their general's prompting, so they danced around in the way the chambermaid dances with the laird at the annual servants' ball.

The general, with a short and stubby finger, feeling at peace with the world, kept time with the music, as the two Frenchmen slowly and formally circled the floor with their overwhelmed partners. In a minute or so — long before the dance would be over — the French would stop dancing, bow, excuse themselves and return to their table. That would have been the form, but before that could happen two surly Quartermaster sergeants went up to the Bambino and two more went up to his friend, the other officer, and the tenor of their remark was, "Beat it, Mac. Go on, get off the floor."

The Frenchmen, still smiling, rather puzzled, but thinking that it was somehow something they had missed, expostulated humorously, but they were hustled to the side of the dance floor and two sergeants took over their girls, laughing scornfully at the perturbation that their partners expressed.

The two Frenchmen returned to the table, where all their companions were eager to laugh it off but for the brigadier. His stubby finger was no longer beating time. He sat up straight, and brought the proprietor over with a look that would have brought a dead man walking. In Italian — in rapid, good Italian, that Angus and Harland only just kept up with — he asked the proprietor to bring to the table the top sergeant of the Americans, and in a moment or so the proprietor returned with him.

The top sergeant was a good-looking youngster, tall, loosely built, and he spoke French fluently, for as soon as he came up he said, standing easily in front of the brigadier. "What is it you wish, general?"

By this time, although the dance was going along merrily, a hush, rather a tense hush, had fallen over the table of officers. As far as Angus could make out, the general said. "You speak French?" and the sergeant said that he did, that he had graduated from college with a major in it. Hell, he was quite prepared to shoot the bull with the old buzzard if that was what he wanted. Then the general said, slowly and distinctly, but in a way that brooked no denying, "When you speak to a general officer you stand to attention in any army, sergeant," and that brought up the loose college boy, who had joined the Quartermaster Corps for the wrong reason, as straight as a ramrod. Angus, thinking back on it, thought the grizzled old brigadier could probably have straightened out a corkscrew with that manner of his. Then, turning to Angus, the brigadier said, with an embarrassed smile and shrug for breaking up the evening. "Why was that, Englishman?" And he gestured to the dance floor.

Almost automatically, because of the earlier pleasant argument that he had had with Harland, Angus said, "I am not English, general, I am Canadian," and then, recovering himself, he looked up at the sergeant and said, "Say, sergeant, what was the idea of ordering those two French officers off the floor? They weren't trying to steal your women; they were just trying to be friendly."

The sergeant, rigidly at attention, was assuming a sulky, set look. "Well, sir," he said, "we paid for the band," and he let his voice trail away.

Angus felt embarrassed, but he turned around to the

brigadier and said, "General, the Americans paid for the music," and he shrugged his shoulders.

The old tough brigadier looked at him for a moment sadly, and then he half muttered, fingering the cloth of his American shirt, "Yes, that is true; the Americans did pay for the music." For a moment he sat there thinking; then, taking a deep breath, he got to his feet and shouted almost gaily at his entourage, but with a sort of command. "We're leaving now!" and turning formally toward Angus and toward Harland, having put on his round French cap, he saluted and said, "Good evening, Americans!" and he marched out, right through the dance, with his men behind him, who did not seek the eyes of Angus or of Harland, following their leader.

They all marched out right through the dance, and the band stopped playing as they left, and the dancers stood around in little knots. A cloud came up over the moon, and Angus shivered a little as he called for cognac for himself and Harland. The sergeant had relaxed by this time, and he came over and stood embarrassedly by the pair of them.

"Hell, sir," he said to Angus, to both of them. "I didn't mean that, not that way. They could have stayed if they wanted to."

Angus looked at him, with the joy gone out of him, and he swallowed down the cognac straight. It tasted like gasoline. "Sure, sergeant, sure you didn't mean it; and, hell, you have paid for the band." He waved his hand over Naples Bay, at all the war, at all the years after. "It's all going to be your band, and you're all going to pay for it, God help you."

Leaving Harland still sitting there, Angus started walking downhill toward Sorrento. He didn't feel American any more, wishing that he did.

*PRAY FOR THE WRITER*